Don't Even Think It

HELEN ORME

Rans⚹m

Don't Even Think It

HELEN ORME

Series Editor: Peter Lancett

Published by Ransom Publishing Ltd.
51 Southgate Street, Winchester, Hampshire SO23 9EH, UK
www.ransom.co.uk

ISBN 978 184167 698 2

First published in 2008
Copyright © 2008 Ransom Publishing Ltd.
Cover by Flame Design, Cape Town, South Africa

Before writing full-time, Helen
taught for nearly 30 years in
a large comprehensive school
as a special needs coordinator.
Don't Even Think It is informed
by many years of working with
damaged and troubled young
people.

At the last count she had
published over 70 titles. When
she isn't writing she runs writing
workshops for teachers and
children.

IN THE SAME SERIES

Seeing Red
PETER LANCETT

The Questions Within
TERESA SCHAEFFER

Breaking Dawn
DONNA SHELTON

Marty's Diary
FRANCES CROSS

Don't Even Think It
HELEN ORME

Questions! Everyone keeps asking questions.

So, I found my old diary and read it again. No – **not true**. I didn't find it! I've known all along where it was. I've kept it safe for a long time but haven't read it since... **THAT** day.

Don't know why I'm reading it now. Don't know why I'm writing now, except that there's no one I can tell.

How could I have been so **stupid**! I was a smug little geek – thought everything was wonderful.

I'm going to write all about our family.

What a load of rubbish. Why didn't I **see**? It was so **obvious**!

I could have **stopped** it! I could have done **something**!

Am I going to start writing again? **No way!** Am I going to keep this? Don't know!

Don't Even Think It

What's the point? What's the point in anything any more?

Questions – always questions!

It makes me sick!

What **am** I going to do?

Abigail's Diary

January 1st
I got this diary for Christmas, so my New Year's resolution is to write in it every day.

Mum says that lots of famous people kept diaries and it's a **good thing**! Mum's always telling me what things are **good things** to do – it's because she's a teacher.

She says a good way to start a diary is to write about our family and what we do and the things we like. She says I can put other things in my diary to make it interesting – like pictures or postcards.

It's the sales in town so Mum took us to look round. Mel spent some of her money on new clothes. Dad **didn't approve** but Mum said they were OK.

I bought a box to keep my diary in – it's got a lock so I can keep it hidden from Mel. I might want to write things about her!

January 2nd

So – about our family. There's me – Abigail – I'm the youngest. I was twelve in November. My birthday's the 20th. Melanie is my **big** sister. She's a **teenager** – her birthday is in April and she'll be fourteen. She goes to The Lord Stanley Comprehensive and she's in year nine. She's got blonde hair and is tall and pretty. She takes after Dad. I've got brown hair and I'm short. I take after Mum. Mum is a teacher at Mel's school. She teaches English – **worse luck!** – and is Head of Year 10.

Dad is more fun than Mum. (Don't get stressed if you read this Mum – I know you are always busy.) He takes us swimming and to play tennis. He's sporty and **healthy** and goes on about eating the right sorts of things. He likes to take us for long walks in the country in the summer. He's an accountant. Most days he goes to work in his office, but sometimes he stays at home and works on his computer.

Boring day today. Mel went out with her friends Luce and Gemma. Mum was busy working – *I can't take you out today – I must make a start on my paperwork.*

Dad said he'd take me swimming if I wanted, but in case he hadn't noticed it's freezing! Stayed in to read some of my new Christmas books. I've still got three to go.

January 3rd
Anyway, more about me. My best friend is Alison. She's in my class at school. Our teacher is Ms James. She's quite young and quite good fun. Alison's got two older brothers who go to Mum's school, and a baby sister (Karen). Jimmy is in year eight. He moved on to Lord Stanley at the beginning

of this year. Our schools are a bit funny – you don't move on until the end of year seven. He fancies Mel, but she thinks he's weird and won't talk to him. Brian is 16 and brainy. He ignores us most of the time.

I like reading, some sporty things, and playing computer games. Ali's got a console which is much better than an ordinary computer. At school I'm best at writing – I don't tell mum, but I quite like writing stories as well as reading them. Sometimes I write horror stories. Horror and ghost stories are my favourites to read. I got this book for Christmas called **Real Life Hauntings.** It's about ghosts in all sorts of places – not just castles and things, but in ordinary places like pubs and houses. There's even a haunted bus station! I've lent it to Ali. We are going to see if we can find any haunted places near us.

January 4th
We all started back at school today. Mum had to go in yesterday – of course – for a training day. Dad stayed at home and went and bought

a new computer. It's really good – a flat screen with great speakers. He says he really needs to do lots of research on the net. He's given Mel and me his old one, but it's going in Mel's room, so I bet she'll **never** let me use it!

January 8th

I don't think I can write everyday – too boring. So what have we done? Not much really, so I'll write a bit more about us. Our house is quite big. We've got four bedrooms and a big garden. Ali's house is quite close – just down the road, which is good.

Mum's always been a teacher. She used to be really good fun, but she got this new job last year and now she's always working. She likes walking, like dad, and gardening, but she almost never goes on long walks any more. She's always got *too much to do*.

Dad is really great. Ali says she likes him more than her dad. He's younger than her dad. He plays with us when he's home and he gives Ali cuddles and makes a big fuss of her.

He's nice to Luce and Gemma too, but sometimes he gets really cross about the way they dress. Sometimes he is a real pain when he goes on about **being decent.**

My Grandma and Grandpa live about an hour's drive away so we get to see them quite often. I wish they lived closer. Ali's got three grandparents and they all live quite close. She's got lots of aunts and uncles close by too. I wish I had – she gets loads more presents at Christmas 'cos she's got so many people to get them from.

Grandma and Grandpa are Mum's parents. She's an only child so no aunties there!

I've never met my other Grandpa. That's Dad's dad. Dad won't talk about him. My other Grandma died when Dad was quite little and he doesn't say much about her either. I only know about them at all 'cos we had to do a family tree in school once.

Dad's got one brother, my uncle Alan, but I've never met him either. I asked Mum about him once, but she said that Dad didn't like his family much and so he hasn't seen any of them for years. Not since he's been a grown-up. She says it doesn't matter though 'cos he's got all of us to love him.

January 9th
I told Mel about the ghosts. She said there are no such things as ghosts. I said she should prove it, but she just laughed. I think she's **WRONG**. My book says that some ghosts you can see, but others you can only hear or feel. I would **really** like to see one.

January 14th
It snowed last night. It was good fun at school. We made a slide in the playground. It was great until Mr Jones (He's the caretaker and a real misery) slipped on it. Then he went and told Mrs Kellet (our head teacher – pretty nice most of the time). The trouble was we all saw it and laughed at him so it made him really cross. So we all got sent in and he went off to the shop to

buy a big packet of salt. Then Ms James decided that it would make a good science lesson to talk about salt and melting points. Why is it teachers **always** want to make a lesson out of **everything**?

Mum was really grouchy when **she** got home. She doesn't like snow – at least not on school days. She says it makes things too difficult. She was really moany when she got in and had a row with Dad. It was all her fault really. She is a real misery sometimes. She went off to bed even before I did!

Dad got a DVD for me and Mel. He went off to work on his computer for most of the evening. He shuts us out these days. Mel went in to see if he wanted a cup of coffee, but he shouted at her because she was disturbing his work.

Ali and I have got a really **GOOD IDEA**. We are going to be a ghost-hunting club.

Tomorrow we are going to go into town to the library and find out about haunted places near us.

January 15th

Dad is nearly as mean as Mum. I wanted to use the Internet to find out about ghosts so I went into the study early this morning. When dad saw me at his computer he went **ballistic**. He says I've got to use the old one, but Mel won't let me go in her room most of the time. Anyway she was in bed. I don't see why I can't use the new one. Dad never minded before. He said he was going to keep the door locked. Mum said that that was silly, but he did it anyway and they had another **big** row. I suppose it's all my fault this time.

It had snowed again in the night. I wanted Mel to come out into the garden and help me build a snowman, but she said she didn't have time, and anyway it's too childish! Why are they all so **MEAN**? Maybe it is childish, but it's fun.

Mel went out early. Mum and Dad sort of made things up. I went round to Ali's and we went to the library. We had to go to the local history bit. The old woman at the desk was a bit funny, but we told her we were doing a project for school so she had to let us in. It was really good. We found lots of books about ghosts but they won't let you take them home. We are going to go after school on Monday and make lots of notes.

January 16th
Good day today. Dad took us for a walk in the woods. Mum came too. Had a good snowball fight. Even Mum enjoyed it. She hadn't got too much work to do tonight and she wasn't tired, so Dad didn't go off into the study.

January 17th
Good news! We have found out that there are three places near us that are **definitely** haunted. The church has got **two** ghosts. It's quite a new church. They had their centenary about five years ago so we didn't think it would have any, but it was built on top of a very old church. There used to be a crypt – a big hole underneath for the bodies – that got filled in and one ghost is a monk who walks through the church and sinks

into the ground because he walks down the steps into the crypt. The steps aren't there any more, but he doesn't know that.

The other is a lady who walks round and round the churchyard at midnight. She murdered her baby and now she has to look for the place it's buried. She goes out looking every time there's a full moon!

There's a ghost near the old railway station too. It's a man who jumped in front of a train. He's a soldier from the First World War. The book says he comes out of the station building and looks up and down the line, then he jumps. The book says he caused an accident once when a train driver saw him and stopped his engine so fast that parts of the train came off the rails and crashed into the platform. Some people were killed – I wonder why **they** don't haunt the station too. It would be great if we could see him.

The third place is in the woods. No one has seen the ghost but lots of people say they have heard screams. They say that a young girl was murdered there – years and years ago when the woods were really thick. No one could get killed there now – there aren't any thick bits and too many people.

January 18th
We told Jimmy what we'd found out and asked him if he wanted to be in our club but he just laughed at us. We'll show him! We are going to find one of the ghosts.

January 20th
It was Mum's birthday yesterday. She is forty! That's really old. I think she **feels** old. She got a load of cards. I got her some perfume. Mel bought her a really big pot for the garden. She went with Dad after school on Tuesday and they bought it and hid it in the shed. Dad got a load of flowers. He hid those in the study – he had to lock the door to make sure Mum didn't go in, but she was too tired to bother anyway. That's not her real present. Dad's arranged a surprise party for tomorrow night. Mel and I are going to do the food. Mum's often late home

on Friday nights 'cos she *tries to get things sorted for Monday morning*. Dad's going to pick us both up after school and take us into town to buy everything.

January 22nd

Mum didn't like it! We all worked really hard. We got lots of food and Dad got the drink. He said we could both stay downstairs until nine o'clock then we had to go up to our rooms. We decorated the house – we got balloons and party poppers and one of those banner things.

We had everything ready when she got back. At first she thought it was good, but when she saw how much food there was she went sort of funny. When Dad explained about the party she got really cross. She said she was *much too tired* to cope with a lot of dad's *smart friends*. Then Dad got cross too and said that she *never appreciated what he tried to do for her*. So then she said *if it means so much to you then* and put on that look that means she'll do whatever it is but **won't be happy about it**.

I thought she looked pretty when she was dressed up and she seemed to enjoy it when everybody got there. It **wasn't** just Dad's friends but hers as well.

They all had a lot to drink (saw the bottles this morning) and made a lot of noise.

She was cross again this morning, so Mel said we would do the clearing up. That made Dad pleased anyway!

January 28th
Haven't done much this week. We went to the old station after school on Tuesday, but there wasn't anything to see. You can't even tell it was a station.

Yesterday we went and looked at the church. It was really creepy when you got round the corner from the floodlights. The trouble was the door was locked. We really wanted to see the old monk but it's no good if we can't get in. We thought about the woods, but it's too far to walk after school.

Mum and Dad are still having rows. He says she's working too hard and never takes any notice of him. She says he should be *more understanding*.

I talked to Mel about it. She said that *they are just going through a bad patch*. She says I'm too young to understand and *we've got to let them sort it out for themselves*.

January 29th

I'm sick of the rows at home! I've told Ali all about it and she says I can go round to her house whenever I like. Then they can get on with it.

We have been making PLANS. Ali's got a new camera. She got it for Christmas. It's a digital one and we are going to take some photos. We are going to concentrate on the lady who has to look for her baby. We are going to wait until the next full moon and then we're going to go at midnight. We've got it all planned.

February 3rd
Mel was off school today. She said she'd
got 'flu! Mum said that it was only a cold
and she ought to go, but Dad said he would
take the day off to look after her so she
could stay at home. Mum got shirty but
she said she *hadn't got time to argue about
it*.

When I got home Mel was in bed, so she
must have been really ill. I tried to go to see
her, but she wouldn't let me in.

She wouldn't talk to Mum. She shut her
bedroom door in Mum's face and wouldn't
come out. So Mum got cross with her and
said she had to go to school tomorrow.

Later I heard Mel crying, but she still
wouldn't talk to me or come out. I don't
know what's wrong with her. She doesn't
usually make so much fuss when she's ill.

February 4th
Mel went back to school today. Dad said
he'd stay at home if she wanted. Mum told

Dad she didn't care and she *hadn't got time to sort out Mel.* She went off really, really early. Mel looked as if she'd been awake all night and her eyes were all puffy as if she'd been crying. She said she **didn't** want to stay at home. Dad said she ought to stay, but she just ignored him, grabbed her bags and went off. She got home from school late, but as Mum was even later she didn't get told off. She went out this evening and it was really late when she got in. I heard her talking to Dad. I bet he was moaning about her being out so late.

February 5th

Mel is a **real cow**. She was in a right mood again this morning. I was trying to tell her about the new plans Ali and I had made to look for ghosts in the churchyard. She just snapped my head off. She looked awful and I told her so.

Mum was in a bad mood too. She's been taking her sleeping pills **again**. She looked all white and sleepy. The only person in a good mood – except me – was Dad. He asked if we wanted to go swimming. When will he learn about winter? Mel said she was going out with Luce and Gemma. Dad said he didn't like Luce and that she's a *bad influence*. That means he thinks her skirts are too short and she wears too much make-up. I said I was going out with Ali and he told me to be careful! Does he think I'm a kid? He said I had to take my phone. Mum didn't say anything much.

We went to the church again, but it was no good at all. It was freezing cold and the churchyard was full of drunks. The church was still all locked-up. We are **not** going to give up. It's going to have to be the full moon, midnight and the lady. Went to the library and got some books on ghost hunting. They might help.

It was horrible when I got home. Mum and Dad had been having a row. Mum had been crying. She tried to pretend that she was alright but I could see that she wasn't. She is no fun these days. She moans all the time and she keeps going on and on at dad. I don't know how he stands it.

She went to bed early again. At least it meant a peaceful evening. Mel rang at tea-time and said she wouldn't be back 'til late so it was just me and Dad.

February 7th

Mel was in a bad mood **again**. She wouldn't sit with me on the bus going to school. She sat all on her own. When I asked her what was the matter she just told me to shut up – so I did.

Went round to Ali's after school. Her mum said I could stay for tea. We had a good time.

When I got back Dad was in the study working on the computer. He switched it off when I went in. Mum was late home again and Mel was even later. Mum had a go at her because she hadn't let her know she would be late. Mel said she didn't like coming home when she would be on her own. She knew Mum was going to be late so she went out with her friends. Mum told her she was pathetic so she rushed off to her room. I went up to see her. She was just lying on her bed all curled up and cuddling her old teddy bear. I asked what was the matter, but she wouldn't tell me.

I wish they would all stop being so miserable.

February 8th

Mel is **still** being a misery. She had another row with Mum this morning and rushed out of the house **hours** before bus time. Dad wanted me to go with her, but I hadn't finished breakfast. Mum just shrugged her shoulders and said that Mel was an *adolescent and what did he expect.* She said she was *dealing with this sort of thing all the time at work and she wasn't going to get into it all at home.*

When I got to the bus stop Mel was talking to a man. She pretended she didn't know me, so I just ignored her back.

Went round to Ali's for tea. Jimmy had got this really, really good horror DVD. Ali's mum and dad hadn't got back from work so we sneaked the DVD up to her room to watch. Her mum didn't get back until six o'clock so we watched it all. It had got to the bit where it was really scary – the **thing** was prowling outside the house looking for a way in – when there was this scratching noise on the window. We both screamed and Jimmy came rushing in. He said we all ought to go and look outside to see if there was anything out there. I didn't want to go!

When we got outside Jimmy kept saying *Look Out!* and things like that so we went back in **fast!** We put the DVD on again, but then the noise on the window happened **again!**

Ali ran out of her room screaming and Brian came to see what was happening. We told him all about the noises and he went straight into Jimmy's room. He grabbed Jimmy and made him tell what he'd been doing. Jimmy had got an old garden broom – one of the ones made of twigs – and he'd leaned right out of his window to reach round to Ali's window. He is so **immature!**

Dad came to pick me up at hometime. I was glad I didn't have to walk in the dark. I know the noises were only Jimmy, but **you never know what might be out there!**

February 10th
Our house is haunted! **Brilliant!**

I told Ali all about it and we decided on a **plan**. We have tried to find a ghost in all sorts of places and now we've got one of our own. I wonder why it has just started to haunt us?

I heard it last night. First there were footsteps outside my bedroom door. Then there was a strange creaking noise. I thought that something was going to come into my room and I hid my head under the duvet, but nothing happened. I didn't dare get out of bed. Then I could hear moaning, then more footsteps, very quiet. After that I could hear sobbing noises. These are all things that the books say are **signs**. The book says you have to look for **cold spots**. When you find one, **that's** where the ghost walks.

Ali got her garden thermometer and we put it by my bedroom door. I had to put it in my bedroom and hide it behind my school bag. We really wanted to put it on the landing but I bet Mum would've found it and wanted to know *what's this?* – she is **soooo** nosy. She always wants to know about **everything** we do.

February 12th

The thermometer didn't show any cold spots. Maybe it's the wrong type of thermometer. But I heard the noises again last night. I'm surprised that Mum and Dad didn't hear them, but I suppose Dad was downstairs on the Internet again and Mum's taking her sleeping pills **all the time.** They keep on having rows about Dad spending so much time in the study on the computer. Mum goes off to bed and crashes out, so what does she expect him to do?

The noises were just the same. Footsteps and moaning. I didn't hear the crying noises though. I tried to ask Mel if she'd heard anything. She wouldn't talk to me again. She went out early and didn't get back until 11 o'clock. Dad was **soooo** cross. I could hear him shouting at her even though they'd sent me to bed ages before.

February 14th, Valentine's Day

I got a Valentine. I think Ali sent it. Mel got three – none of them signed. Dad sent one to Mum, but she didn't send him one.

It's half-term but Mum said she had to go in to school. She asked Dad if he could work from home any time this week, but he said he couldn't. Mum was annoyed, but she said she'd come home at lunchtime and that Mel had to look after me. I don't know why everyone keeps saying I need looking after. I wanted to go round to Ali's, but Mum said I had to stay at home so Ali came around here.

We are going to go to the churchyard **TOMORROW** night. It's a week until the full moon and we want to **make our plans**.

Mel went out this afternoon. I asked where she was going but she wouldn't tell me. She said I wasn't to say anything to Mum or Dad or she would **kill me!** She got home before them so there wasn't a problem. One funny thing though – Luce rang here for her. I thought she was out with Luce and Gemma. Luce said she'd texted loads of times but Mel hadn't answered. I told Mel, but she just said she had other friends and it's not anything to do with me. She said to keep my nose out. If that's how she wants to be – tough! I don't care what she's doing.

February 15th
It worked **brilliantly**. I told Mum I was going round to Ali's and she told her mum she was coming here. We decided half past six was a bit early for the churchyard – even this time of year there will be too many people around – so we went to Jan's Cafe instead. Mum doesn't like us to go there really so I was cross when we got there and I saw Mel. She was with the man from the bus stop. She didn't look very pleased to see me either so I just ignored her. Mum would

be really cross if she knew Mel was hanging around with a strange man so she's not going to tell on me.

It was just after eight o'clock when we got to the church. It was a bit cold. The floodlights were still on, but we got in by the side gate. There's a great big tomb near it with a tree growing close to it. I think it's called a yew tree. It was huge and the ground underneath was quite dry. Ali had brought her camera.

We could see most of the churchyard which was good. There was a crack in the tomb. Ali said maybe there were vampires. Next time we come I'm going to bring Mum's jar of garlic powder. That should keep them away.

Then we heard the noises. We thought it **must** be the ghost. Ali poked her camera up over the tomb and got a picture. It had such a bright flash we thought that it would frighten the ghost away. **Then** this awful wailing noise started. We got really scared. Ali grabbed me so hard I nearly screamed out loud, even though I knew it was her.

We didn't dare move in case it got us. We sat really still for ages. I needed the loo – badly – and I thought we were never going to get away. **Then** there was a panting sort of noise and footsteps and running sounds. As soon as the footsteps went away we made a dash for it out of the gate.

Maybe we've got a picture of it. I hope so. Ali's going to print it out tomorrow.

It was really late when I got in and Dad was in a strop! He'd rung Ali's house and knew I hadn't been there. Mum was in bed again but Dad said she knew all about it.

Then Mel came in and he started on at her so I went to bed.

February 16th
Mum had a go at both of us this morning. She wanted to know where we'd both been. I said that Ali and I had just been walking around, talking. I didn't say anything about Mel. Mel told Mum to mind her own business – so I got away while she was freaking out at her.

Bad news! Ali has had to tell her dad what we were doing. They weren't **too** bad about it. Her dad thought it was a bit of a joke, but we're not to go out late at night again. **THIS DOES NOT AFFECT OUR PLAN!**

But what's worse is that our ghost photo was **Jimmy!** He thought it would be funny to follow us and give us a fright. He had to admit it because we showed him the print. He said we were braver than he'd thought!

But we know just what to do next week at *MIDNIGHT.*

We've still got the ghost in our house. We're going to concentrate on that. We need a new plan for now.

February 18th
Ali brought her camera round so we could have a practice with it. It's very easy and the best thing is you can just stick it up from wherever you're hiding and get a picture.

She left it behind when she went home so I could have a go.

Mum, Dad and Mel had a **big row** because they wouldn't let her go out. I wasn't allowed out either. I don't care. I've lots to get ready.

February 19th

It was really weird last night. I wanted to try to get a picture of the ghost if it came again so I stayed awake for **ages** waiting for everyone to go to bed. Mum was first – sleeping pills again! Then Mel came up. I don't know what she was doing. She sounded as if she was moving her room round. Then I went to sleep! **How stupid can you get!**

I woke up because there was a noise. There was a sort of scraping sound. I got out of bed and grabbed the camera. I opened the door just a crack so I could get the camera round and take the picture. Then I nearly died! **Something** grabbed my hand. I thought it was the ghost!

Turned out it was **Dad!**

Don't Even Think It

I don't know what he was doing wandering around at that time of night (That's what they always say to me when I get out of bed!) and without putting the light on. It's enough to scare any ghost away. He came in and tucked me up in bed. He asked what I was doing and I told him about the noises. I didn't say anything about ghosts. He sat down on my bed. He was all hot and sweaty and I didn't really want to be cuddled. I wish they would **stop treating me like a child!**

He told me I *wasn't to worry about noises* (As If!) and I was to *go back to sleep.*

I pretended to, but I didn't. I heard him go back to their room, but then the sobbing noise started again. It was very quiet, but I **know** I heard it.

Met up with Ali. Her mum took us into town to the shopping centre. We've got to be **looked after** in case we stay out late again. Ali's parents are quite cool though. They haven't made as much fuss as mine.

Mel was still in bed when I left. So was Mum. They are **sooo** boring!

Ali's mum took us for lunch. She's into healthy eating so we went to this quite posh place where she said the food was organic. It was quite nice. I had soup and risotto. After lunch she said we could have a couple of hours by ourselves 'cos she wanted to go to the library and go grocery shopping. We had to promise to **be good!**

We were just mooching around waiting for her to come back when we saw Mel. She was snogging **that man**. Ali's mum saw her too. She gave the sort of look that parents do when there's going to be **trouble!**

February 22nd

Back at school this week. Didn't have time to write yesterday. Ali told me that her mum had asked her about Mel and the man. Ali didn't really know anything about him. She didn't say we'd seen them before. Her mum said she was worried 'cos he looked a lot older and she said she thought she ought to tell Mum. Ali said I should warn Mel.

Mel didn't come home after school yesterday. She didn't get back until nearly 11 o'clock. Mum was going spare. Dad went out to look for her – he drove around in the car for ages, but didn't find her. I got sent to bed, but I couldn't sleep. I just put out the light. When Mel got home I went downstairs and listened at the door.

Mum called Mel all sorts of names. She knew about the man. She said Mel was stupid. Dad tried to calm things down but Mum wouldn't listen to him. She just screamed at Mel and Mel screamed back. I've never heard Mel talk like it before. She sounded really wild. She kept saying mum *didn't understand* and if she did she *wouldn't be going on at her like this.*

Then there was the sound of a slap. I don't know who hit who 'cos I thought it was time to get back upstairs. Just as well 'cos Mum came rushing out of the room, upstairs into her room and slammed the door.

I got back into bed, but I could still hear Mel shouting and Dad's voice. He must have got her calmed down in the end 'cos after a while it all went quiet. Then Mel came upstairs and Dad went into the study.

I don't like it.

I wish we could get back to how things were. It's all Mel's fault – she's really changed and I don't like her much any more. She won't talk to me – she shuts herself away and she's deliberately winding up Mum and Dad.

February 23rd

Mum has been taking her pills again. She looked awful. She made Dad call the school and say she wouldn't be in. When they called Mel for breakfast she didn't answer. Dad sent me up to get her but she wasn't there. Mum got hysterical but Dad told her to calm down. He said *not to worry* and that he would *sort it all out*.

When I got to the bus stop Mel was there. She was waiting for me. She grabbed me and shook me. She said it was all my fault. She said I had told Mum. She really hurt me. She wouldn't listen to anything I said. Then the man came so she left me alone and went off with him.

She came home straight after school tonight. She went up to her room so I went after her. I told her it wasn't me who had told Mum and she started to cry. She said she knew that. It had been one of her teachers. He'd seen her on Saturday and he'd told Mum. He knew the man – he used to teach him. He told mum he was bad – he'd been in trouble with the police. Mel said he wasn't bad at all – it had just been a kids thing.

His name is Jonah and he's twenty, so Mel says he's not too old at all. She said he's the only person she can talk to. I said that she could talk to me, but she just said I was *too young* and I *wouldn't understand*! – she's as bad as Mum and Dad!

She said Jonah lives with his mum. He never liked school – which is why he got into trouble so often – but he knows a lot of things about wildlife and stuff like that. She says he's really gentle and he always tries to help animals if he finds one that's been hurt. He doesn't like the people he was at school with – he got bullied a lot at school – so he doesn't have any friends locally. But he likes Mel. She said she wasn't really snogging him – she just kissed him because he'd been really kind to her.

He goes away quite often – he doesn't like being in one place too long. When it gets to be warmer, he's going to go on the road and she's going to go with him. She says she can't stand it here any more.

I know things aren't good, but it's not that bad. Dad's OK most of the time. Mum gets stressed – it's just her job. Mel should understand!

I don't want her to go away.

February 25th
All this fuss at home has made it hard to plan our next Ghost Hunting Expedition.

The parents keep **checking-up** on us. We are going to go tomorrow.

Mel has been a bit happier the last couple of days. She's going for a sleepover with Luce tomorrow night so she won't be around to bother me.

I'm going to ring Ali on her mobile when it's safe to get out and we're going to meet at the end of the road. I'm going to take Dad's big torch.

February 26th
It all worked well to begin with. Mum went to bed early again. Dad sent me upstairs early too 'cos he'd got a lot of work to do on the computer. I took the spare backdoor key and hid it. I put my alarm on for eleven o'clock. Dad was still working on the computer and I thought he might hear if I went through the kitchen. The light was on in the study, but the door was shut so I crept past really quietly and got out of the window of the downstairs loo. I left it open so I could climb back in when I got back. It's

quite easy if you climb onto the dustbin. It was still open when I got home so I didn't even try the door.

It was really misty, and cold, and I was a bit scared until I saw Ali. It took us ages to get to the church and we kept hearing strange noises. When we got there the lights were all off and it was really dark. We crept round the wall so we were hidden from the churchyard. We got in through the side gate again and hid under the tree. It was hard to see anything because of the mist. We got really cold.

Suddenly we heard a noise – a shuffling sort of sound. Then we saw something white moving along the path! It disappeared before we could take a picture. Then the awful thing happened. The white thing came from behind us and something grabbed Ali!

She screamed really loudly and so did I.

Then the white thing flapped again and started to laugh. Yeah, it was Jimmy. **Again!**

Then it got even **worse.** Someone must have heard us screaming 'cos we heard a door open and a man was coming towards us. We got out of there really fast and ran all the way home.

I think it didn't work 'cos it wasn't midnight. We must have been too late 'cos it took so long to get there.

We are just going to have to **DO SOMETHING** about Jimmy.

February 27th
Good job it was Sunday today. I didn't want to get up this morning. Went with Dad to pick up Mel. He didn't want me to go, but Mum said he had to 'cos she wanted to do some cleaning. Don't know why he didn't want to take me. I got him to drop me off at Ali's on the way home. We had a go at Jimmy and told him he'd got to be **serious**. He thinks it could be fun so he's going to help us. We are going to try again soon – Jimmy says we need a good clear night. It will be better with him coming too. It

might not be so scary. I lost the torch. I must have dropped it when he grabbed us. He says we can go look for it after school tomorrow and he will come with us and we can all have a good look round and see if we can find any evidence.

February 28th

Went back to the churchyard after school. We were a bit later 'cos we had to wait for Jimmy. I went home and left a note for Mum. I said I was with Ali and Jimmy and I **WOULDN'T BE LATE** for tea. Mel wasn't back. When Jimmy got back home he told Brian he was going to be looking after us so Brian said he'd tell their mum. Jimmy said it would be ok if we were with him.

We found the torch under the tree. Then we saw that someone else was there. It was Mel – with Jonah. They were sitting in the church porch and he had his arm round her. She was crying and they didn't see us.

A man came around the side of the church and asked us what we were doing. Jimmy told him we were doing some research for our local history project. He didn't look as if he believed us but he didn't say anything.

March 4th
Busy this week. Didn't have time to write before. Jimmy says we need to be organised. We've got to keep notes. I don't know how I will have time to write notes about our ghost as well as write my diary. I don't want to write my ghost diary here 'cos this is private and I don't want anyone to see it. Not even Ali.

I'm going to **TRACK** our ghost here at home. Jimmy says Ali can do the church ghosts. At least I can use this diary to work out when I've heard it before. Jimmy says to keep a note of the time and then I can work out when it's going to come again. He says that it might be a **LOST SOUL.** He says these ghosts haunt you for a bit then go away again. We've got to find out how old our house is and what was here before.

March 5th

It came again last night. It was at a quarter to one. I heard very quiet footsteps and then the sobbing. Jimmy says I need to find out about its **ROUTE**. I can't work out where it's going. It sounded as if it was going towards Mum and Dad's room. The sobbing came after the footsteps though. I don't want to go out of my room.

Grandma and Grandpa are coming over tomorrow. Mum was busy cooking and cleaning.

Mel stayed out all day, but she came home quite early, so there wasn't a row.

March 6th

We had a good day. Mum was pleased to see Grandma. She always makes a big fuss of Mum and tells her not to work too hard and things like that.

I told Grandpa about our ghost. (Not about the one here – the one in the church.) He said he had something in a book about the church and he would send it to me. He said that it was only stories and I wasn't to start to *really believe it and get frightened*. He likes local history and he says it's a good way to find out about things if you read about old legends.

March 10th

Lots to report! Jimmy and Ali and I had a meeting after school. I got the letter from Grandpa – he photocopied some pages from his book about the history of our church. Jimmy has found out that the church isn't always kept locked. He says we can go in on Saturday afternoons – we are going to go this week.

I showed him my list of times when I've heard our ghost. It hasn't always come at the same time – sometimes it's been about midnight, sometimes later. Most times I heard the sobbing noises but sometimes there were groans and other noises. Jimmy says to make sure I write everything down.

Here's the stuff Grandpa sent.

The Church of St Lawrence was built just after the turn of the 19th century. However there are several interesting features, most notably the crypt which dates back to the monastic foundation of the fifteenth century. The monastery was deliberately destroyed during the Reformation. Local people, roused by tales of greed and licentiousness, set fire to the monastery one hot August night. A small group of monks took refuge in the crypt but the church buildings collapsed, blocking the exit, and the monks were buried alive.

A later church was built on the same site but repeated tales of sightings of ghostly cowled figures frightened churchgoers and by the end of the 17th century the church was deserted by the congregation.

During much of the 18th century the church buildings were left to decay, with local people taking much of the stonework to incorporate into their house building. However the church grounds continued to be used as a burial ground. The north-west corner was used as the pauper ground. Needless to say there are few tombstones or other tangible relics here.

During the building of the new church in 1901, the crypt was discovered and the jumbled bones of several individuals were found.

During the early years of the 20th century reports of ghostly sightings, although fewer in number, continued to circulate. In addition to stories of monks there is a 'white lady' who is reputed to haunt the graveyard looking for her baby. The baby, born in the local workhouse, was taken from the mother at birth and sent to a baby farmer. The child soon died under mysterious circumstances. This was a common occurrence at that time when unwanted children were 'disposed' of at a very early age. The distraught mother supposedly took her own life, but as a suicide was buried outside the consecrated ground. Her ghost has, allegedly, been seeking the child's burial place for the last hundred or so years.

A further twist to the ghostly tales is added by reports of hauntings of nearby houses. It is claimed that those families who used the old stones as building material have been troubled by strange noises in the night. These include ghostly footsteps and, in some cases, noises, allegedly the screams and cries of some monks, unable to find shelter in the crypt, as they were burnt to death.

I showed it to Ali and Jimmy. Jimmy says we've got to **prioritise.** He says we must go to look at the church and see if we can find the crypt. We are going to meet up there on Saturday.

The story of the lady is different from the one we found in the library, but I don't know how we can find out what is real.

Jimmy thinks that maybe our house has got some of these stones. Ali says we should look in the garden 'cos that's where people put fancy stones.

March 11th

Mum was really late home again. There was some sort of meeting after school. Dad was late too. Mel said she was going to stay the night with Luce again. She grabbed her stuff and just went. Mum moaned at me when I gave her the message, but it's **not my fault.** She tried to ring Luce's house to check, but there was no answer. She got me to text Mel – just to check she was OK. Mel texted back – she said Luce's mum had taken them out and not to worry – she'd be back tomorrow. I don't think Mum was very pleased.

No ghostly noises in the night.

March 12th
It was a horrible day.

Mel didn't come home this morning. Mum rang Luce's house again and there was still no answer. Then she rang Gemma's mum. **She** said she thought that Luce and her family were away for the weekend! She asked Gemma if she knew what was going on, but she didn't. Gemma said she hasn't seen much of Mel lately – except at school.

Mum and Dad were really worried. They tried to ring Mel on her mobile, but she didn't answer. But then she sent me a text saying to tell them she was OK and she'd be back tonight. They calmed down a bit when I showed them the message, but they were still cross.

They made a bit of a fuss when I said I was going to see Ali, but Mum said I could go if I rang a couple of times to let them know what I was doing. This is Mel's fault – she's doing her own thing and I get them taking it out on me.

We had arranged to meet at the church at four o'clock. Jimmy said it would be quiet by then. I went earlier though – I couldn't stand it at home any longer.

It started to rain while I was getting to the church and I got all soggy. Jimmy was right though – it **was** open. The door was heavy and difficult to move but I got in OK. The church wasn't like it is when you go for weddings and things. There were hardly any lights on and it was really spooky.

It was only two o'clock, but I didn't want to go out in the rain so I thought I'd have a look around and see if I could find anything interesting before Jimmy and Ali arrived. There were lots of doors but they were all locked. I thought I'd have a look at the floor. There was nothing in the main bit, but over in one corner I found a slab that was all worn down one edge. I had to get right down on the floor between the pews to look at it properly. It was very dark and I could hardly see.

Then there was a noise. It was the door opening. I knew it wasn't Ali and Jimmy and I was scared, so I slid right under the pew so that no one would see me.

Then I got such a shock that I nearly sat up. I heard Mel's voice. I looked out under the rows of seats. I couldn't work out at first who she was with. I was going to get out 'cos I thought she couldn't tell on me. She's in enough trouble anyway – but then I heard what she was saying and I thought I'd better stay where I was.

She was with Jonah. Mum and Dad would kill her if they knew. She's been told not to hang around with him.

I don't **really** know what she was on about but it sounded serious. **I have my suspicions!**

She was crying all over him and saying things like – *I can't tell Mum, she just wouldn't believe me* and *I don't know what to do.*

She said she was scared and she doesn't want to be at home.

I think she's been having sex with Jonah and she's scared of being found out. There was a girl in her class who got pregnant – I heard Mum talking to Dad about it.

I hope she's **NOT** pregnant. Mum would go **demented**!

I didn't know what to do – I just stayed there. The floor was **very** hard! After a bit it got even darker and then there was this flash of light. I thought it was the ghost, but then I heard the thunder.

Mel and Jonah must have decided to get out 'cos I heard the door slam. I waited for a bit but there was no noise so I got out from under the pew. I was all dirty where the muck from the floor had stuck to my wet clothes. It was half past three and I really wanted to go home. I thought I'd better ring Mum and let her know I was OK. Then I texted Ali. She sent a message back to say they couldn't come! Their mum wouldn't let them out because of the storm and because they couldn't think of a good reason to tell her why they wanted to go out. At first I was cross – I thought she could have texted me earlier. Then I thought it was a good thing she hadn't 'cos Mel might have heard. I don't know what she would have done if she'd found me.

I don't know what to do. Should I tell Mel that I know? She's so funny about everything these days.

I got soaked going home. Luckily Dad was in the study and Mum was busy working too, so I got in without any questions.

Mel still not home.

March 13th
Mel got in really late again. Mum had stayed up and they both went on about where she'd been. I went downstairs to listen. Mel had to

admit that she knew that Luce wasn't there. She wouldn't tell them where she'd been. She just kept saying *around* and *none of your business.*

They kept on for ages and I went back upstairs. I heard Mel come up – she slammed her door hard. Then Mum came up too. Dad went into the study. I waited for a bit until they all settled down, then I thought I'd go see Mel.

I was as quiet as I could be and I opened the door really carefully. When I went in I thought she would sit up, but she just made a funny noise and sort of cuddled herself into a ball. She kept saying *No, Please,* over and over again.

She sat up when I spoke to her though and told me to get out. I said I wanted to help her. She made a snorting sort of noise and said that no one could help. She told me to go away.

Today Mum and Dad got us both together for a **long talk**. Mum tried her head of year *I am your friend* bit. Dad was being 'specially kind and gentle too. We got all the stuff about we *worry about you* and *you are old enough to be responsible now* and Mel got a load of *you can trust us if you've got problems.*

Later, Dad said that he's going to book a holiday for Easter. He wants to go abroad but Mum said she couldn't *face the flights* so they've decided we will have a cottage somewhere instead.

March 16th

Dad took us swimming after school today. Mel said she didn't want to go but Mum said she had to. She was going to be late home **again**, and she didn't want Mel **left on her own!** Mel came along, but she sulked **all** the time. She is such a miserable cow these days. She's just no fun any more.

Jimmy came round to our house later. He's got a leaflet about the church and it gives times when you can go in. We are going to look for the crypt again and for the place where the baby might be buried. I'm **not** going by myself though.

March 17th

Heard our ghost again last night – just the same – footsteps and moans then crying noises.

Wrote down all the details in my ghost book.

March 19th

Told Jimmy our ghost came again. He says we need to find out about the history of our house. We had a look in the garden to see if there might be stones from the old church. There are lots of stones in the rockery, but the little ones are just ordinary and we couldn't move the big ones very easily. Jimmy turned one over using a crowbar from the garage, but then Mum noticed what we were doing and came out and yelled at us. I didn't know what to tell her, but Jimmy said we were looking for buried treasure. He told her that he had been reading about the Romans and thought there might be a Roman hoard under the stones.

Mum laughed then and said that it wasn't very likely as the house was only twenty years old. This means that the house can't have been built from bits of the old church. So why is it haunted?

Jimmy went home then and Ali stayed – but she wouldn't come up to my bedroom. I don't see why she made so much fuss about it. It's not my room that's haunted – it's the rest of the house. She kept on about the ghost. I wish she hadn't. It's made me feel all creepy.

March 20th
Heard the ghost **again** last night. I can't really see a pattern to the times it comes. Maybe it comes every night, but I don't always hear it.

Mel was really moody again this morning. She got up early – she **never** does on Sundays – and went out before breakfast. She's not in yet so there'll be another row.

Don't Even Think It

March 21st

Mel didn't come home **at all** last night! It was awful. Dad and Mum had a big row about what to do. Mum said they should call the police, but Dad said that that would be silly. They both stayed up all night and kept going to the door and opening it.

Mel came back at about half past six this morning. They both started on at her – asking *where was she?* and things like that. Mum said *was she with THAT BOY?* Mel said that she wasn't, but wouldn't tell them where she'd been. She said that *she couldn't bear it in this house.* Mum screamed *What do you mean?* Mel shouted back *You don't want to know.* Dad tried to calm things down, but he had to shout to make himself heard. Then Mel came out of the sitting room and ran upstairs. I went out to see her, but she just pushed me out of the way. She got dressed in her school uniform and rushed out again. *One day I'm going and I'm never coming back again ever!* she yelled as she went out.

Mum wanted Dad to go after her, but he wouldn't. He said it was better to leave her alone and said that he would talk to her when we all got home. She came back at about half past nine tonight. I got sent to bed. I tried not to listen but they all made so much noise that I couldn't help it. Mel's not being allowed out at all. Mum is going to take her to school and bring her home again. She said she wasn't going to let her out of her sight.

I don't understand. Why is Mel being like this? I know that Mum's a pain sometimes, but she was worried about Mel! So was I. And Dad's great, except when he and Mum have been fighting. If Mel wasn't being so stupid they wouldn't keep going on at her all the time. It's all her own fault really.

March 23rd
Jimmy was waiting for us when we got out of school today. Wednesday is one of the days when the church is open. We had a good look around. Jimmy had brought some money and we bought a guide book. The guide book has some stuff about the history of the church **AND** a plan of it. It's got something about

them discovering the crypt, but it doesn't say anything about ghosts. The plan shows where the crypt is though – it wasn't the hole in the ground I thought. The entrance is outside, so we might see the ghost even if the church is shut up.

A man came and asked us what we were doing – Jimmy said we were doing a local history project. It's a good excuse. The only trouble was, the man wanted to know what the project was all about and he talked to us for ages.

Jimmy asked him about burials. He showed us the oldest part of the churchyard. We asked him about the ghost of the monk, but he laughed and said that there are no such things as ghosts.

Mel has shut herself up in her room. She won't even come out for meals. Mum is still **furious** with her. I tried to go talk to her. I think I should tell her I know all about her and Jonah. When I went in, she was curled up on her bed. She was crying – she sounded just like the ghost. She wouldn't talk at all.

March 25th
It's the end of term. We are going on holiday tomorrow. I shan't take this with me 'cos there won't be anywhere to hide it.

We shall be away for April Fools' Day – Jimmy told me a joke to play. He said he did it to his mum and dad one year. He said you have to get a load of clingfilm and put it all over the loo – under the seat! He was creasing up laughing just telling me about it. He said it worked brilliantly – when his mum got up in the morning she didn't notice at all until her feet got wet! He said I should try it. Ali said it was OK, but Jimmy had got into a lot of trouble – his mum didn't see the joke – and he'd had to clean it all up! Jimmy said it was worth it just to hear what his mum said. I'm not sure I'll try that one, but I'll think of something else.

April 1st, April Fools' Day!
Didn't play any jokes on anyone – no one was in the mood.

Back early – we should have stayed until tomorrow.

We went to Cornwall.

We had a cottage – it was quite small and Mel and I had to share a room. I thought she'd moan, but she seemed quite happy about it.

The first few days were great. Mel was in a good mood and she did things with me, even though she sometimes pulled faces when I suggested things.

It was really cold in the sea so Dad bought us both wet suits. Mum said it was a waste of money, but Dad said it would be good for us. They're funny things and you still feel cold at first, but you do get warmer after a bit.

Mum said she was having a *good rest*. She'd brought a load of books and sat and read a lot. Sometimes she stayed at the cottage while we went down to the beach with Dad.

Anyway, everything was going great until yesterday. Dad wanted to go for a long walk. Mum wanted to stay in and read and so did I, so Dad said Mel should go with him. She didn't really want to go, but he kept on at her until she said she would. They were gone quite a long time then Dad came in carrying Mel. She'd fallen down some rocks and hurt herself quite badly. The side of her face was all red and lumpy and she'd done something to her arm. Worst were her legs and back. She'd got deep scrapes where she'd been cut by the rock.

Mum wanted to take her to the doctor straight away, but Dad said it was too late. He said the best thing would be to come straight home. So we packed up and drove back overnight. They made up the back seat so it was like a sort of bed for me and Mel, and took it in turns to drive.

We got back in the middle of the night. They put us straight to bed.

This morning Mel stayed in bed. Dad went in to see her and kept saying he was sorry, over and over again. He told Mum he felt guilty and that it was his fault, but Mum said not to be daft. She said Mel was old enough to know better and that she should have been more careful. She still wanted to take Mel to the doctor, but Dad said he didn't think it was serious – she hadn't broken anything or hit her head. Mel didn't want to go either so Mum gave in.

April 2nd

Mel said she feels a bit better, but she still aches all over. I asked her what had happened. She said she just slipped on the rocks and fell down. She wouldn't tell me any more. She's gone back to being really miserable. She's been lying around all day. Dad is still making a big fuss over her.

April 3rd, Easter Sunday

I got three big eggs and a box of chocolates. Mel got one egg and a gold chain from Dad. I think he got it for her 'cos he still feels bad about her accident. She's still miserable.

Dad keeps on about how he still feels bad. He keeps going to find Mel and asking her how she is and saying he's sorry. He keeps trying to cuddle her but she says she hurts too much. Mum is getting a bit cross with him, I think. She asked Mel if she wanted to go to the hospital to be checked-up, but Mel said no – she *just doesn't want to be fussed at!*

April 4th, Bank Holiday

Some bank holiday! Mum and Dad both worked all day. Dad said *it's too busy on the roads to go out.* Mum said *I need to make a start on my work.* I wanted to go round to Ali but her family had all gone out for the day.

Mel shut herself in her room for most of the day. Dad locked himself in the study all day and worked on the computer. Mum went upstairs to *work in peace.* I couldn't even go to the library 'cos it's shut.

April 5th

Ali came round this morning. Mel went out. I don't think she was supposed to, but Dad had gone back to work and she got out while Mum was upstairs working.

Ali says Jimmy says we need to go and look at the old part of the graveyard. She says he went on his own while I was away and he found a bit where the baby might be buried. It's outside the main churchyard. There's a sort of shed there where they keep the mower and gardening tools. She said that Jimmy said that there are all sorts of lumps in the ground that are the graves of people who were buried outside the consecrated ground. That means not in the churchyard – like in the stuff Grandpa sent. He wants us all to go late at night again.

Mel came back at tea time. Mum had a bit of a moan, but she said she'd been with Gemma and told Mum to ring if she didn't believe her – **so Mum did!** How embarrassing can she be? I'd die if she checked-up on me like that. Anyway Gemma's mum said she'd been there all day, so Mum didn't go on too much. They've been nicer to Mel since her accident.

April 7th

Now I'm in **real** trouble. They said I was *as bad as Mel.* They said *I wasn't to be trusted* and they *don't know what to do with either of us.* **It's all Jimmy's fault!**

Yesterday he decided we needed to go back to the church at midnight. He had been looking around and said we could get into the shed. He said the baby was sure to be buried there, so it was our best chance of seeing the lady. Ali rang me to say they would be at the end of the road. It was quite hard to get out without Mum or Dad seeing, but I managed OK – I got out of the window again. It wasn't as dark in the street and not as scary as last time. We had to go right through all the graves and **that** was spooky. Jimmy showed us how to go into the shadows and run from one hiding place to another. He knew how to open the door and we all got into the shed. Jimmy said that he would keep watch through the door and we could look through the window.

I nearly died when it happened. Suddenly there was a bright light and the shed door came open with a crash. It was a man. Jimmy yelled **run!** and pushed him out of the way. He tried to grab Jimmy, but Jimmy was too fast. Then he grabbed at my arm, but I got away. Ali got out while he was trying to get me. Jimmy yelled to split up so we all ran different ways. I had to come home all by myself.

Ali came round this morning and told me what had happened to them. The man chased her – she is the slowest runner – and nearly caught her, but Jimmy got behind the man and pushed him so he fell over. They thought that they were going to escape, but he was a fast runner and he caught Ali again. Jimmy had to go back for her. The man was really cross and shouted all sorts of things at them. He made them tell him their names and where they lived.

The worst part was later this afternoon. Mel had been allowed out with Gemma again. (Mum had checked up to make sure.) I stayed in and read my book. Then there was someone at the door. Mum looked out and said *Now What?* It was a policeman. I thought it was something about Mel – so did Mum – but it wasn't! It was about **ME!** The man who came to the shed last night had gone to the police. He said that there was a gang of kids who kept hanging around the church and that last night they had broken into the shed to steal things. Now I'm grounded and I'm not allowed to go round to Ali's until Mum has been to talk to her mum!

April 11th
Back to school today.

It was a horrible weekend. I wasn't allowed out at all. Mum is more stressed than ever. Dad's cool now – I told the police all about our club so Mum and Dad found out about it all. Dad said it's fine, but we shouldn't listen to everything Jimmy says. He says we should stick to finding out things in the library and stay away from the church for a bit. They both said *no more creeping out at night* so I had to promise. Dad said Mum will calm down in a bit. He said she's worried about Mel and I should try to *make things easier for her* and not get into any more trouble.

At least the police believed what we told them. Ali says Jimmy is in the most trouble 'cos her mum and dad blame him. She told them it was our idea, but they still say Jimmy *should have had more sense!*

April 14th
Jimmy is cross with us. He says it's all Ali's fault! **Cheek!** He was the one who suggested the shed. Ali says he's not going to help us any more. Good job too. We didn't want him in the first place. **AND** he's taken over all our plans. We talked about what to do next. We are going to give up for a bit. We thought about the woods, but they are too far. Anyway, now it's the summer term there is going to be sports club after school.

April 16th
I heard our ghost late last night again. I wish it would stop. It's not fun any more.

April 17th
It's Mel's birthday next week. She wanted

a sleepover but Mum said she can't cope. She says she's too busy at school to organise anything, so Dad said that he would take Mel and Gemma and Luce bowling, then they could go somewhere posh to eat. I said I wanted to go too, but Dad said that it was Mel's birthday and it was going to be a grown-up thing now she's fourteen. I'm going to be allowed to go round to Ali's for the night – so long as I promise to **BE GOOD**!

Dad and Mum had a row. Mum says Dad is spending *too much time* on the Internet. She says *he knows how busy she is* and how he *should be supporting her*. She says she can't see why he has to *spend so much time shut away* and he *stays up too late at night*. He said he *doesn't know why she's moaning. He needs to work too* and anyway *she never knows when he's in bed or not because of her pills*.He said *she takes too many pills,* but she says she *can't cope without them*.

Then they both started having a go at Mel saying that the way she behaves makes things worse for them both. I got out before they could start on me.

April 19th
Went swimming after school tonight.

April 21st
Ali's mum has had a good idea. She said we ought to go play tennis in the park. She has booked us a court each Thursday for six weeks. She took us today, but we can go on our own next time because it's not far to go.

April 23rd
Mel's birthday.

April 24th
Had a great time at Ali's last night. Jimmy says he's forgiven us for dropping him in it. Cheek! It wasn't our fault! He said their mum and dad have got over it all and they aren't cross any more.

I heard Ali's mum talking to her dad. She was talking about Mel. She said that she thought they ought to get me round to their house a bit more. That would be good.

Stayed until quite late, then Ali and her dad walked home with me.

There had been another row. They were all cross when I got home. **Something had happened at bowling that Mum didn't like**. I think it was something Dad did, but I don't know what. Mel looked as if she had been crying and so did Mum.

I asked Mel later if she'd had a good time. She said it had been OK to begin with but Dad had spoiled it. She wouldn't say why. Mum didn't go because she had work to do. She took them to the bowling and went to pick them all up later, so that Dad could have a drink. She was going to take Gemma and Luce home, but they wouldn't wait and had got a taxi by themselves.

April 25th
Mum's in hospital!

She's going to be all right, but she's got to stay in for a little while – We don't know how long.

April 26th

Ali's mum said I could go and stay with her while Mum's in hospital if I want to. Dad said I could go, but later on Mel asked me not to go. She said she doesn't want to stay at home all by herself.

So – what happened? Yesterday Mum overslept. She had had a load of sleeping pills again. She was in a mad rush 'cos she needed to get to school and just threw her things into her car and drove off.

The police came even before we had left home. We all went to the hospital and waited there until they said she was OK. She doesn't remember anything about the accident, but the police say that her car went out of control and she went over the wrong side of the road and hit a huge lorry coming the other way. The car's a write-off. Mum was really lucky. The lorry driver was upset but not hurt.

I think she was still sleepy, but Dad says not to say anything to anyone. He told the doctors it's just stress.

April 27th
Grandma came today.

She went to see Mum in hospital and had a long talk with her. She is going to stay with us until Mum is out of hospital.

Mel is really pleased.

April 28th
Played tennis with Ali after school. Grandma said that Ali could come and have tea with us afterwards. She asked Mel if she wanted to have her friends round, but Mel says they don't come here any more.

Grandma wanted to know if she had fallen out with them, but Mel said that they had just got other things to do.

I wonder why she said that. Maybe it's something to do with what happened on her birthday.

April 29th
Mel was allowed out tonight. Grandma doesn't know about all the fuss and Dad had gone to see Mum. He didn't look very pleased when he got home and Mel wasn't here, but he didn't say anything in front of Grandma. Mel came home quite early. Luce and Gemma had walked home with her – I heard them saying goodbye – but they didn't come in.

April 30th
It has been nice having Grandma living with us. She visits Mum in the day and stays at home with us in the evenings while Dad goes to see Mum. He has stopped working so hard and doesn't go into the study so much.

Mel is happier now. Maybe it's because everyone's thinking about Mum instead of going on at her.

We've been in to see Mum most days. She says she's feeling better now and *thinking straight again*. I don't know what that means.

May 1st
Grandpa came today. Mum is supposed to be coming out of hospital tomorrow. She's not going back to school straight away. She's going to go and stay with Grandma until she feels she can cope at home. Dad will take us to see her at weekends.

May 2nd, Bank Holiday
Mum came home from hospital today. She says she feels *fragile,* but a lot better. They are going to go back to Grandma's house tomorrow.

Mel said could she go too, but Dad told her *of course not* – Grandma needed *to focus on Mum* and anyway *we mustn't do anything to worry Mum.*

May 3rd
We had to say goodbye to Mum early this morning and then go to school as usual. We don't know when she will be back. Dad says it depends on how quickly she recovers. He said she's not to rush back too soon.

May 5th
Tennis after school. Saw Mel – with Jonah – in the park.

Dad was back when I got home. He says he's going to have the rest of the week off, then he's going to work mornings only, so he's here when we get home.

Mel has been a bit happier the last few days. I told her I'd seen her with Jonah in the park. She said that they had to meet in the park 'cos they couldn't go to the church any more. She said there's always someone around there now – ever since they caught us. She said she wished she could have gone with Mum. She said she doesn't like it without Mum and could she come and sleep in my room. I said had she heard the ghost? She gave me a funny look and said she just didn't like her room any more. Maybe she has been hearing it too and is scared as well. I would quite like her sleeping with me.

We went and got one of the garden loungers out of the garage and took it up to my room. Dad wanted to know what we were doing, so we said we wanted to be together for a bit. I didn't tell him about the ghost. He said we were being a bit childish, He knew we were upset about Mum, but we *really didn't need to go to these lengths.* He seemed quite cross. I don't know why.

May 6th

It was fun having Mel sharing with me. She was back like she used to be. She talked a bit about Jonah. I've promised not to say anything to **anyone.**

There were **no** noises in the night.

May 8th

We went to Grandma's house yesterday and stayed the night. Mum looked OK and she was really pleased to see us. Grandpa asked how the ghost-hunting was going. I didn't want to tell him about the police, so I just said we'd stopped for the summer. I told him about tennis and he took me out into the garden for a game.

Grandma had cooked lots of cakes for tea and she gave us a load to bring home. I was sad to leave Mum. She still can't come home.

May 10th

I like having Mel in my room, but it's a bit difficult to write my diary. I'm going to hide it with my school books and pretend I'm doing homework. It's quite safe 'cos Mel won't want to know what I'm doing, and Dad doesn't check up like Mum does.

Yesterday Dad decided he would take us to school in the car. He dropped me off first. He says he will try to take us as much as possible. I don't see why. It's just as easy to get the bus.

Mel was late home again. I had been round to Ali's for tea and she still wasn't back when I got home. Dad didn't seem worried though – I thought he might have been cross. She got in about half past nine and said she was going straight to bed.

Dad sent me up soon after. Mel was in bed and asleep. (I don't think she was really – she was just pretending 'cos she didn't want to talk.)

May 11th

I woke up in the night and thought it was the ghost again, but it wasn't. It was Mel was crying. I asked her what the matter was but she didn't answer.

Dad said he'd take us to school in the car again, but Mel wouldn't go. I think it's because she wants to meet Jonah on the bus. If Dad knew she was still seeing Jonah he would really hit the roof.

May 12th

Tennis tonight. Went back to Ali's for tea. Jimmy asked what was wrong with Mel. I said she was just in a bit of a mood again. Jimmy said he didn't mean her moods – he said she hadn't been at school since Monday. He said he asked Luce where she was, but Luce had told him that there were problems at home and it's none of his business. He said he knew about the problems, but when he said about Mum, Luce just made a rude noise and told him not to interfere when he didn't understand.

May 13th
Mel woke me up in the night again. She was making noises in her sleep. She kept on saying *No! No!*. Then she was going on about Dad. I couldn't really understand what she was saying. Then she started making moaning noises as if she had a pain.

She was sick this morning when she got up. She suddenly went all white and rushed off to the bathroom and I could hear her throwing up. Maybe she isn't very well. **Or maybe what I thought before was right.**

Dad made us go to school in the car again today. Mel said she didn't want to go, but he said it was more convenient for him and we had to. I wonder if he suspects Mel has been bunking off.

May 15th
Went to Grandma's again. Mum looks better – she is going to stay one more week and come home next weekend. It was a good weekend. **Everyone was happy!**

May 16th
Dad says he's going to go back to work – he's just going to try to get home early each day. He says I can go round to Ali's each day after school and come home at tea time.

May 18th
Mel was crying again in the night. I asked her what was wrong – I thought she wouldn't answer me, but she told me that Jonah had gone. I didn't know what she meant at first, but she said he's gone to work with a fair, travelling round the country. She doesn't know when she'll see him again. She said she *really needs him to be with her*. I nearly asked her if she was pregnant!

May 19th
Tennis tonight and tea at Ali's house.
Jimmy says that Mel still hasn't been to
school. He says that her form tutor thinks
she's gone with Mum. I don't know how he
knows that!

I don't know where Mel goes each day
– I think she used to be with Jonah, but
now he's gone she can't be. She's started
getting up really early so I don't know if
she's still being sick. She goes back into her
own room and does things on the computer.
She's told Dad that she's doing coursework
for school. I don't see why if she's not going
to school.

Should I tell Dad she's not going? She'll
kill me if I do, but I'm really worried. Maybe
it will be better when Mum gets home. She'll
have to go to school then.

May 20th
Dad came up to my room after tea and
moved all Mel's things. He says we've *got to
get things tidy for when Mum gets back.*

When Mel came back she went spare! She said she wanted to stay with me, but Dad said she couldn't. She did though – very late she came in with her pillows and loads of cushions and slept on the floor. She's weird.

Heard the noises in the night. It's ages since I heard them. Footsteps again and then a door shutting. No crying sounds. Mel **must** have heard. I'm sure she woke up too.

May 21st
Mum's home! Hooray! She's much better, but she's not going to go back to school until after half term.

May 22nd
We had a barbecue to celebrate. Mum said Ali could come and told Mel to invite Gemma and Luce, but they couldn't come.

Dad says he's going to sleep in the spare room. He says he doesn't want to disturb Mum in the night if he works late. She's not taking her sleeping pills any more.

May 25th

Footsteps in the night again. Sounds of doors opening. I opened my door just a very little bit. It was Dad! What a relief!

There haven't been many noises lately. Maybe we haven't got a ghost at all. Anyway I'm bored with ghosts. Ali and me think we might take up archaeology. It was Jimmy's idea. He thought of it when we were digging up the rockery. He's going to use some of his savings to buy a metal detector.

Mel in a mood again. She went out very early. She wouldn't talk to Mum or Dad.

May 26th

It's the last day today. We get tomorrow off for a teachers' training day. Mum's going in for the day to get used to being back at work without any kids around!

Tennis as usual. I'm getting really good now. I beat Ali six-three. Jimmy turned up half-way through the game and started trying to put us off. Ali says that's why I managed to beat her!

Jimmy is so stupid, but he makes me laugh. First he started making monkey noises. Then, when we didn't take any notice, he started trying to climb the netting around the courts. That was what Ali reckons put her off. The netting isn't very strong and when he tried to climb it, it just shook and he ended up falling off. So he pretended that he was knocked out – then Ali got her water bottle and chucked it all over him. **That was really funny!** He went away then and left us alone.

May 27th
Mum was **sooo** cross when she got home! She's found out about Mel! Dad had come home early so she told him all about it – she was cross with him 'cos she said it was *his fault and he should have looked after us better!*

Dad said it wasn't. He said he had *done everything he could.* He said he'd taken us to school and everything, and it wasn't his fault if Mel didn't go. He said Mum's accident was her *own fault*. If she hadn't taken so many pills she wouldn't have had the accident. Mum started to cry so Dad calmed down a bit.

Mum said Dad had to have a long talk with Mel. She said that people at school had told her that Mel was still seeing Jonah. She said *he had to sort it out* because she *couldn't cope at the moment*.

Dad promised that he would. He asked me if I knew anything about things. I said that I thought Jonah had gone and that Mel was really unhappy because she missed him. I didn't know what else to say. Should I tell them about her getting pregnant? It might not be true – but I know she's been sick again, AND she isn't eating very much. He asked if Mel talked to me and told me things. I said no, but he might talk to Luce and Gemma. Then he said *not to worry – it'll all be OK*.

May 28th

There was another awful row when Mel got in last night. I could hear it all. I stayed in my room and left the door open just a bit. Mum and Mel were yelling. Dad kept trying to make them calm down.

Mel had to tell them some of the things she'd been doing. She said she hated school and that no one wanted to be friends with her any more. She told Dad that it was all his fault. I can't understand why she blames Dad. Mum said *what did she mean?*, Mel said *ask Dad – he knows.*

Then they started on about Jonah. Dad didn't let on that I'd said he had gone, so she can't say it's all my fault. They wanted to know where she'd been. She said *around,* but they wanted all the details. She's been in the woods – Jonah's got an old car and he met her each day around the corner from school and they drove out there.

Then Mum said *had she been having sex with Jonah* 'cos if she had she was going to go to the *police.*

Mel really flipped. She said *No Way* would she have sex – *It was horrible and disgusting.* She sounded as if she were telling the truth. Maybe she's not pregnant.

Mum said that she would take Mel to the doctor's and find out for certain, but Dad said that he believed Mel and *that wouldn't be necessary.*

Mel said that they were all wrong about Jonah. She said that no one had ever given him a chance. He just didn't like the things that people like Mum think are important. She said that he is her friend and she likes being with him. She told them that Jonah had gone away so they needn't try to get him done by the police 'cos she wouldn't see him anyway.

I don't think Mum believed her but they sent her to bed after that.

May 29th
Dad went into Mel early this morning. I heard the footsteps, but I knew it wasn't

ghosts or anything because it was daylight. I wanted to know what was going on so I opened my door and sat just behind it. They were talking really quietly – I suppose Dad didn't want to wake up Mum or me.

Mel said that nothing was going on with Jonah. Dad called her his little sweetheart and kept saying that he was sorry, and how much he loved her. I could hear Mel crying, but then I couldn't hear what Dad was saying.

Then Dad started talking about Mum and not worrying her. He told Mel she's not strong, she mustn't have any nasty shocks and we don't want to upset her. Mel started to cry even louder so I went back to bed. I wonder if there's more wrong with Mum than they're telling us.

Later on Mum and Dad both had a talk with Mel. She didn't shout at them and she's promised to go to school. Mum doesn't want her to get into too much trouble so she's going to try to fix things if Mel stays good until the end of term – it's quite a long time though.

Dad's going to take us both to school again. He says Ali can come with us if I like. I asked if Jimmy could come too, but he said no.

Anyway, it's half-term now and we are going to do things as a family for the week.

May 30th
Dad's got some time off work. He took Mel and me out for the day. He said Mum needed to rest. We went to Watervale Park. It's about an hour's drive from home and it's really good. I thought Mel might say she's too grown up for it now, but she enjoyed it too (at first). Dad even bought us candyfloss **(I love candyfloss)** which he won't usually 'cos its not **healthy** and he let us buy burger and chips at lunchtime. He usually goes mad if we ask for burgers, but he was being really, really nice. He kept making a big fuss of Mel and cuddling her and asking if she's alright. I think he feels bad because of the things Mum said about her.

She didn't like it when he put his arm round her and kept pushing him away. When

I asked what was the matter she just shrugged and said it's kids stuff and she's too old now. So then she got into another strop. Nothing makes her happy these days and she's so selfish. She spoils it all for me too.

June 1st

I went round to Ali's for the day and her Mum took us and Jimmy and Karen swimming, and then into town. She bought us lunch – healthy stuff today! Karen is quite good at eating now, but when we got up to leave there was a ring of food all round the table. Ali's mum looked at it and said *Now there's another place we shan't be able to come to for years!*.

Mel wasn't allowed to do anything but Dad said he'd take her out later if she wanted. She wouldn't go though. Mum's calmed down a bit, but she's still cross with Mel and won't talk to her much. Mel's trying to be really nice to her too.

Jimmy bought his metal detector. He was cross when he got it out of the shop because he couldn't start using it straight away. He hadn't realised that they had batteries and you had to charge them up. He says he's sure he will be able to find treasure. He said he'd like to go back to the churchyard, but Ali and I aren't going if he does. Anyway his mum says he's *to stay well away – they wouldn't be very keen on him digging up the graves!*. She said he needs a large field or somewhere like that – but *not the park or playing field!*. Jimmy said he might try the woods. He says he can get there easily on his bike – but he didn't say that to his mum!

June 3rd

Mel is still being sick. I wonder if she's **anorexic.** We saw a telly programme about eating disorders – it said sometimes teenage girls make themselves sick. She's not really fat though.

Dad took us out again. We went for a whole day hike. We took a picnic. I watched Mel – she didn't eat very much.

June 4th
There were noises in the night again last night. I didn't get up. I don't know what they are. Sometimes it's Dad – I think it might be Mel too.

We are all going to Grandma's house for the day tomorrow.

June 5th
Had a good day today. Mum went and had a talk with Grandma. I think she was telling her about Mel.

June 6th
Back to school today – Dad took us. Mel said Mum was waiting at the gates when Dad dropped her off. That won't last long – Mum will soon be **too busy!**

June 8th
Went to Mel's room to use the computer. I wanted to use it for my topic work at school. I couldn't make it work – Mel's put a password

on it! I asked Dad if I could use his, but he wouldn't let me. I'm going to have to do it all in handwriting. They are ALL so mean.

June 21st

I'm really worried about Mel. She's getting texts from Jonah – I wish I knew what they mean. I found out 'cos Mum made me take her phone. I went round to Ali's after school. Her mum took us swimming and Mum said she wanted me to ring her when we got to the pool. I forgot to charge my phone so I said could I borrow Mum's? Hers was out too – then she saw Mel had left hers behind and told me to take that. I think Mel had left it behind on purpose so they can't keep checking up on her. Anyway I did.

After swimming it beeped – it was a text. From Jonah! It said – **hang on coming back**.

I didn't text anything back.

After a bit it beeped again – another text. It said – **don't do anything stupid – call me**.

Then again – **answer me**.

I thought I'd better answer so I just texted back **OK**.

I hope Mel doesn't find out. She will though – but it wasn't my fault, Mum made me use it.

June 22nd

Mel had a go at me for reading her messages. I said it was Mum's fault, but she said I didn't have to read them and that they were private. I asked her why Jonah said don't do anything stupid – what was she planning? She said if I didn't know anything I couldn't tell anyone anything. I wonder if she's going to run away – I know she thought about it before. Maybe that's why Jonah's coming back.

She still keeps being sick, though she tries to hide it. I wonder why Mum hasn't noticed.

Dad is still making a big fuss over her. Sometimes he's nicer to her than to Mum.

Mum's getting stressed again. Dad said she should have some time off – he said no one would mind, but she won't.

June 30th
Mel didn't come home tonight. Mum rang everyone she could think of and no one knew anything. We thought she would be back this morning but she wasn't. Mum called the police. Dad didn't want her to, but she said she didn't care what Dad wanted and that he didn't care what happened to Mel. So then they had another row.

Anyway – a police lady came to our house to talk to us all. Dad said I was to *be careful what I said* 'cos *we didn't want anyone to get the wrong idea*. I don't know anything anyway so what could I say?

Mum told the police lady about Jonah. She asked if this was the first time Mel had stayed away overnight so they had to say *No*. She said that lots of girls Mel's age do this sort of thing and that she would probably *turn up soon*.

July 1st

She still hasn't come back. I sent her a text, but she didn't answer. Mum got on to the police again. They are still saying not to worry.

I sent another text saying that they knew about Jonah and Mum had got the police involved.

July 2nd

She's back! The police found her – but only by accident! She was chucked off a train 'cos she didn't have a ticket. There was a policeman on duty who started asking questions – she gave her own name and he recognised it. They brought her home in a police car.

She told me about it later. She said it was thanks to me – she was pleased with me. She said that it was a good thing I had warned her, because she was with Jonah. He'd met her from school on Thursday and taken her to where he's working. She said when she got my text about the police she decided she'd better come home 'cos she didn't want to get Jonah into trouble.

She told the police that it was just a row at home and they went on a bit about wasting police time.

Mel says next time she's going to do it properly. She said she hadn't meant to do it this time – it was just that when she got in the car with Jonah she knew she wanted to get away from here. Next time she's going to make sure she's got money and clothes then she won't ever have to come back.

I asked her why she wanted to leave – she just said *she couldn't stay here much longer*.

Why?

July 18th
Nearly the end of term. The summer holidays – hooray. I don't know why I want the holidays though. Everything is so horrible here. I'd rather be at school. Mum and Dad and Mel spend **all** the time moaning and fighting with each other. Dad says he's fed up with both of them. Mind you, he still makes

more fuss of Mel than anyone else. He keeps buying her presents and being extra nice to her even when she's in one of her moods. I wish he'd buy things for me.

July 20th
It's been awful!

Mel hasn't come home **again.**

Dad insisted on taking us to school this morning. Mum was cross when she got in tonight. Mel hadn't been into school today. Dad said he'd *done his bit* and dropped her off at school this morning. Mum asked if he'd seen her go in. He said he'd stopped before they got to the school gates 'cos she didn't want people to see her being taken to school by her dad. He said he hadn't stopped because he'd wanted to drive into town as he needed some new shoes.

So then she had a go at Dad and started blaming him for the way Mel behaves. He stamped off to the study and locked the door! He wouldn't come out, not even to eat.

It's after midnight now and Mum and Dad are having another blazing row – I expect it's still about Mel. I wouldn't like to be her!

July 21st, Last day of term

They made me go to school. Mum went in too. Dad said he would come home early from work in case Mel came home. She didn't though.

Mum wants to call the police again but Dad said to wait. He said that it will be like last time and there's no point in getting the police involved.

Mum wasn't happy so she started ringing Mel's friends. They just said that they hadn't really seen much of her for ages and didn't know anything.

Then she got cross with Dad. He was cleaning his car when she got home. He's polished every bit of it – even the wheels! – and got the house vacuum out to clean the inside. He **never** cleans the car – he always gets Mel and me to do it – I suppose he just wanted to do something outside while he was waiting. Mum didn't understand though – she said he ought to have been out looking for Mel.

Mum just went on and on at him about it until he said *if she felt like that she should have had the day off work and done it herself.* So then she said she would, but he said she *wasn't in a fit state to drive* and took all the car keys into the study and locked the door.

Went round to Ali's. I just wanted to get away from Mum. I think I know why Mel wanted to get away. I wish I could! I wonder if she'd let me go and stay with her and Jonah. Mum said not to say anything to Ali's family, but I'd already told Ali. Anyway Jimmy knew she hadn't been at school.

July 22nd
She's still not home. They called the police at tea time yesterday. Dad says he's sure she's OK. He didn't want to get them involved again but Mum wouldn't wait any longer. Of

course they knew she'd gone missing before and Mum **got very stressed** because she said they weren't taking it seriously. She went on about Jonah again. They said they had to give Mel some time to get in touch because of the *history*, but they would see if they could find Jonah. They know she's with him – so do Mum and Dad.

I sent a text again, warning her. It worked last time so maybe she'll listen again.

I know she said that next time she was going for good, so I thought I'd have a look round her room and see what she'd taken. **She hadn't taken anything! No clothes. Nothing!**

She hadn't even taken her favourite coat. She's got her mobile and the purse she takes to school – the one with the long leather strap. I couldn't find her school bag so I expect she's got that, but I thought she was going to take more things. I wonder why she didn't?

Mum came in and asked me what I was doing so I told her I didn't think Mel had taken any stuff. She'll be back in a couple of days. I told Mum not to worry. I said I'd send her a text message. Mum said to tell her she loved her and please come home.

July 23rd
She hasn't sent any messages. I wish she'd answer so I know she's OK. Mum and Dad are both stressing. Mum says we need to tell Grandma. She rang her today and cried a lot. They are going to come tomorrow. Mum rang the police again. They said they are following up reports and looking for Jonah. They said *they'll keep us informed.*

Mum's been cleaning. She's been going all round the house, but she won't go into Mel's room at all. She's shut the door and told me to stay out.

Dad's been out in the garden. He says we all need to *keep busy.* He cleaned out the shed and took a load of stuff to the dump. He threw out a load of old tools and stuff. He used Mum's car to take it 'cos he said he didn't want to get his all messed up again.

Then he made **me** clean Mum's car! He said I needed to keep busy too.

July 24th

Grandma and Grandpa came early today. Grandma looked really worried, but Grandpa said it would all turn out right in the end and not to worry. Dad agreed with him. Mum had to tell Grandma **everything** that had happened. They sent me out into the garden. They didn't want me to hear, but I know a lot more than they think I do.

They decided to stay the night and I went down so I could hear them talking. Mum kept saying that it was all her fault. She said she had been working too hard and not taking enough notice of Mel. Grandma and Dad both told her it wasn't her fault, but she wouldn't take any notice of them.

July 26th

They went home today. They said they'd stay if Mum wanted, but she said she'd be OK. She's not though.

Dad went to work. He said he'd stay at home, but she didn't want him either.

The police came round this morning. They wanted to know if we had heard anything from Mel. I told them that I'd sent a text, but she hadn't replied. They asked me a lot of questions – I think they think I know where she is.

They told Mum that they were still trying to trace Jonah. They had been to his house but his mum said she hadn't seen him for ages and doesn't know where he is. They've suggested that they let the papers and telly know. They said Mum and Dad can do an appeal. That's where the police get them in a big room and they film them asking Mel to come back and saying things like they won't be cross and stuff. I've seen appeals on the telly before. It feels strange when I think they're going to do it for Mel. I wish she would come home. I'm getting really worried. I hope Jonah's looking after her.

I went into her room again to look through her things. I thought she might have left a note or something for me. I tried to get on the computer, but it's still got that silly password and I couldn't get in to it. I tried a few things it might be, but it wouldn't work. I must get Dad to see if he can do it. He knows all about passwords and things.

July 27th

They did the news thing today. Grandma came back to be with me. She looks really worried now too. They told Gran about it afterwards, but they wouldn't let me watch it on the telly.

Mum said it was really horrible. They had to sit on a platform with some police people. Someone had written out some things for Mum to say. She had to ask Mel to get in touch with us. Dad had to say things too. Mum said he was nearly crying as well. They've asked anyone who has seen her to tell them. They said she might be with a man and they'd got a picture of Jonah.

The police say they are certain this will help. They are sure that she will get in touch with us when she sees how upset we all are.

I wish that I had done more to help her. She wouldn't tell me what it was troubling her, but I should have tried harder. When she was sleeping in my room, it was like it used to be. I should have asked her then what was the matter. I wonder if I ought to tell Mum what I know. She might be cross with me for not saying anything before. **I don't know what to do.**

I tried to text again. I told her to come home.

July 28th
Now it's in all the papers. Dad took ours into the study. They wouldn't let me see it. I went round to Ali's and she showed me theirs. I said I wanted to bring it home, but she said they would miss it, so Jimmy went to the local shop and bought three different ones.

This is from one of them...

Fairground Search for Missing Schoolgirl

Desperate search

A desperate search is being carried out to find fourteen-year-old Melanie Winters who has now been missing from home for seven days.

Melanie was last seen when her father, Mark, dropped her off at school on the last day of term. She has not been in touch with her anxious parents since. The family are becoming increasingly worried for her safety.

Fairground searches

Police believe she is currently in hiding with her twenty-year-old boyfriend, John Simms.

Simms is known to be working with a travelling fair. Police sources reveal that they have been checking fairgrounds across the country, however enquires among travelling fairground communities have failed to throw any light on Melanie's whereabouts.

Concerns

They have said that their prime concern is Melanie's safe return to her family and they will treat the runaway couple sympathetically.

Appeal

Melanie's parents, Mark (38) and Kate (40), went public yesterday with an appeal for news of their daughter. In a short emotion-packed speech, Kate begged her daughter to contact the family.

Kate, a teacher at the girl's school, has asked her, 'Just to let us know you're safe'.

The appeal was broadcast on TV in the hope that someone would recognise Melanie or her boyfriend.

Not the first time

Friends of the family have expressed their hope that Melanie will soon be safely home.

'This isn't the first time she's gone missing,' a neighbour said. 'She's a lovely girl, but she's been running wild lately.'

Police confirm that Melanie has gone missing on previous occasions but has always returned after a few days.

Hopes for a happy outcome

Everyone concerned has been hoping for her return, but the police are now intending to step up their enquiries. They have asked for any member of the public with information to contact them as soon as possible.

They all say pretty much the same sorts of things. I don't see why they wouldn't let me see ours. They don't say anything I didn't know.

It feels horrible to see it in the papers though. It makes it seem as if it's not happening to us – it's some other family. Why does it have to be **us**?

I wonder who **the neighbour** was?

When I go out I keep feeling that people are looking at me.

They got it wrong anyway – it wasn't the last day of term, it was the day before.

July 29th

Dad had the day off work today. He said he couldn't face going in. Mum didn't get up so Dad got my breakfast and sat in the kitchen with me. I said I didn't want anything to eat 'cos I felt sick and Dad started to cry. I gave him a cuddle to make it better, but he wouldn't stop. He started to talk about

Mel. He said that *he had loved her and that she had been very precious to him.* He said that *he had always done the best thing for her and tried to make her happy.* He said he *didn't want her to be dead!*

I said *Why should she be dead? She's just gone off with Jonah – everybody knows that!* Dad said he just has this awful feeling about it. He can't tell Mum what he thinks. He said that I mustn't tell Mum either 'cos it will just upset her even more.

He can't mean it! He can't! She mustn't be dead!

They'll find her soon.

I know they will!

July 30th
Ali's going on holiday today. They are going to France. I wish we were going on holiday. I wish Mel would come home. I sent her another text. She still didn't answer.

The police came again today. They wanted to talk to me as well as Mum and Dad. I told them that I had been trying to ring Mel on her mobile and I'd sent lots of messages. The lady said that they had hoped to trace her by checking her mobile, but she hadn't used it since July 19th. That's nearly two weeks!

I had to tell them everything that happened the last time I saw her. I didn't know what to say really. I told them that she had been in a funny mood again that morning and that Dad had insisted on taking us to school, but then I didn't see her again after I got out of the car. She'd made a fuss about Dad taking us and she tried to get out with me. She told Dad she wanted to walk the rest of the way, but he wouldn't let her. Dad told the police lady that it was because he had been worried that if he had let her get out at my school, she wouldn't go to school herself. Then he looked as if he were going to cry. So that made me start to cry too. The police lady was really nice and kind. She told me to call her Annie. She gave me some tissues and said that I wasn't to worry – they just wanted to find out everything they could to help them find Mel. She said that I was really brave, and that everything I could tell them might be important.

They asked me what I knew about Jonah so I told them all the times I had seen them. I told them that I wondered if she were pregnant. I didn't mean to, but I couldn't help it. When I said it, Mum looked as if she were going to faint and Dad made a gasping sort of noise. Annie asked why I thought that, so I told her everything I had been thinking. She said could I remember when I'd first thought it. It was months ago – when we were ghost hunting. I told her about the church but I didn't tell her about the ghosts. I didn't want to get into more trouble about that. She wanted to know why I thought that Mel was pregnant and everything. Then I told them I thought she might have anorexia. Annie asked Mum what she thought, but Mum was crying too and couldn't answer.

Then they wanted to know if Mel had told me anything. I had to tell them that she'd been with Jonah the last time she ran away, but they just nodded – I suppose they'd worked that out already. I told them how I texted her to say that they were looking for her and so she'd come home. I had to tell them that she'd planned it this time. I didn't want to – she'll be so cross with me – but I couldn't help it. **I had to tell them. I want her home!**

Then Annie took me into the kitchen and the policeman stayed to talk to Mum and Dad. I wanted to know what they were saying but I couldn't hear.

When they went, they said not to worry. Annie said I'd been really helpful and they were sure that they would find her safe and well. She said they were going to concentrate on finding Jonah!

July 31st
I couldn't write any more last night so I'm going to carry on now.

Of course, when the police had gone there was a big fuss about all the things I'd said. At first they seemed a bit happier. Mum said that if she were pregnant it would explain everything. Then Mum wanted all the details about Mel being pregnant. I couldn't really remember exactly why I'd thought it. I'm **NOT** going to let on about my diary. It's private and they'll only want to read it if I tell them, so they will just have to make do with what I remember. I told Mum about what I'd heard in the church. Then I told her about what Mel was like when she was away after her accident.

Then Mum got in a state and said it was all her fault that Mel had run away – how she should have been there for her to talk to. Then Dad started on about what he should have done and Mum got cross with him and started shouting that he should have been more supportive to her. Dad said that it wasn't his fault – he said he'd always tried to make Mel happy, so Mum cried even more. Dad said he *wished he could get his hands on that man* and that he'd *kill him for what he'd done to Mel*.

I couldn't stand it any more so I went to bed. I don't feel any happier. None of it's **my** fault!

August 2nd
Dad is being really weird. He came in to see me in the middle of the night. He sat on my bed and kept on asking silly questions like *How are you feeling?* and *Do you miss Mel?* **How does he think I feel? AWFUL!**

Then he started to cry. He kept saying it was all his fault and he should have looked after her better. Then he put his arm round me but he didn't cuddle me like I thought he was going to. He started stroking my arm and then he started to pull at the top of my nightie. When he got close he smelt awful. He had been drinking and it made me feel sick. I pushed him away and told him he ought to go back to bed so he did.

August 5th

It's Dad's birthday today. He's 39. It was an **awful** day again.

Dad sat around most of the day drinking, then went off into the study and shut himself in. Mum just walks round and round the house. She keeps going into Mel's room and then out again. Then she goes to the front door and looks up and down the street.

The police came again in the afternoon and asked a load more questions. They wanted me to tell them more about Jonah. Then they asked about what I was doing in the church that time I heard them talking, so I had to tell them about our ghost hunting. I would have told them about **our** ghost too − but I haven't heard that for weeks now. Maybe because we are all up at night a lot.

Mum hardly sleeps at all. Dad made her take her sleeping pills tonight and took her to bed early. She looks so sad.

I don't know what to do. I wish I could do something to help. I wish I could find Mel for them.

August 6th

Dad came into my room again last night. He is still being weird. I don't like it when he's like this. It makes me scared. He sent me to bed early and said he was going to work. I must have gone to sleep, but he woke me up when he came in. It was like before. He sat on the bed and started talking about Mel and how pretty she was and how much he loved her. Then he got into bed with me. He was all smelly again so I said he was to go away. He put his arm round me and said I had to be nice to him. He said now we hadn't got Mel, he needed me. I pushed at him hard and he knocked my lamp on the floor.

Mum must have heard 'cos I heard their bedroom door open and her footsteps. Dad got out and was tucking me in when Mum came in.

I heard them talking – Dad said I was crying and was all upset. Mum said he should have called her, but he said he didn't want to disturb her when she was sleeping. I wasn't crying at all – why did Dad say that I was?

Dad wanted to take me out today. He said that it would *do me good to get out of the house for a while.* He said he would take me swimming and maybe we could go for a walk in the woods. He kept going on and on about it. I didn't want to go. I don't want to do the things we used to do with Mel. It makes me really sad. Anyway, then Mum started on at me too. She said Dad was right and we had to *try to carry on as usual*! **I wish they would listen to what I want!**

I don't like being on my own with Dad any more. He makes me feel funny – especially when he keeps going on about Mel. I wish he'd leave me alone. I'm not a kid any more. I don't like it when he keeps cuddling and stroking me. They both treat me like a baby.

Anyway, in the end I didn't have to go 'cos Grandma and Grandpa rang and said they were coming over. They stayed quite late.

I went and listened downstairs after they'd sent me to bed. They were talking about Mel again. Mum said she's getting really worried. Dad said that the police have asked them to do another telly thing. Gran cried a lot. She said they'd had people from the newspapers wanting to talk to them.

August 9th
Mum and Dad were on the telly again tonight. Grandma and Grandpa stayed to be with me while they went off and did it. They still won't let me watch.

August 10th
The police have found Jonah!

They've arrested him. They came to tell Mum and Dad today. **But Mel's NOT with him.**

Jonah says that she hasn't been with him at all and that he hasn't heard from her for ages. He got arrested at the bus station.

Why didn't he come in his car?

He **said** he was coming home to see why she hadn't been in touch.

August 11th

It's all in the newspapers again. They've given up trying to hide them from me. Grandma said it would be better if they didn't. I don't like reading them but I need to know what's happening. I'm going to keep them all to show Mel when she comes home. **Then she'll know what we all feel like.** It's really selfish of her. I don't care what she feels – she ought to text me and let me know she's OK. She's been totally selfish for months now – she just thinks she's the only one with problems. **What about me?** What about Jonah – she shouldn't let him have to go to prison. He ought to tell them the truth. Even if Mel doesn't want him to, he still ought to tell them where she is!

Missing Schoolgirl: Boyfriend Arrested

Boyfriend found

Police yesterday confirmed that they had arrested John Simms; the man they have been searching for in relation to the disappearance of schoolgirl Melanie Winters.

Melanie went missing at the end of the summer term and has not been in contact with her frantic parents for three weeks.

Initially police enquiries were focused on local fairs as it was believed that Melanie (14) had run away with the twenty-year-old man known to have been employed as a fairground worker.

However, it is now known that Simms was alone when police found him.

New investigation

A police spokesperson said last night that the investigation has taken a more serious turn. 'It is a great blow to the hopes of all concerned that Melanie was not with this man. We continue to hope that we are dealing with a missing person case, but we have to accept that we may be investigating a more serious crime.'

The police spokesperson refused to elaborate further saying that the police would continue with their enquiries.

Melanie's family were unavailable for comment.

Kind and gentle

Simms' elderly mother said that she was astounded and upset by his arrest.

'I knew he was seeing a younger girl," she said, "but I didn't know that it was the missing lass. He didn't get in touch because he didn't know they were looking for him – he's been in France with his job.'

Mrs Simms says that her son is a kind and gentle person. 'Everybody who knows him likes him. He wouldn't hurt anybody.'

Alternative views

This view of Simms' character is not shared by neighbours who have known the family for many years.

Local residents have described him as 'a layabout' and a 'bit of a thug'. One said that he was 'always in trouble when he was younger, but he's calmed down a bit lately'.

Missing Schoolgirl: Suspect Released

Released

Mark and Kate Winters have to face the fact that the man they believed had enticed away their missing daughter Melanie has been released without charge.

John Simms was arrested two days ago at the local bus station. A nationwide search had been going on for several weeks since the fourteen-year-old schoolgirl was first reported missing.

Long-term relationship

Simms, a twenty-year-old fairground worker, has allegedly had a relationship with Melanie for several months. It is believed that she ran off with him on a previous occasion, although at that time she returned after a few days.

Police initially believed that Melanie had repeated her earlier behaviour and were hopeful that she would soon be home.

The search for the couple was extended countrywide and Mark and Kate made two television appeals for their daughter to contact them.

No contact

Simms was arrested almost as soon as he stepped off the long-distance bus and was taken directly to police headquarters for questioning, but he claims to have been unaware of the search going on for him and his girlfriend. In a statement to the police he has stated that he has not

seen Melanie for several weeks nor had any other contact with her.

He said that he was worried because she hadn't been in touch and only came home to find out why.

He was detained in police custody while enquiries were made into his movements.

Statement confirmed

Police have confirmed that the statements Simms made about his own whereabouts have been confirmed by his employers. There were no reports of anyone having seen him with Melanie, or of Melanie having been seen at any of the places Simms is known to have visited.

Talented girl

Mr and Mrs Winters agreed to a short interview to comment on the most recent developments. 'We had all hoped that she was with this man' said Mrs Winters, fighting back the tears as she spoke. 'It has been a terrible blow to us that she hasn't come home with him.'

Mr Winters, describing his daughter as a beautiful, talented girl said, 'Our lives are on hold at the moment. We can't think of anything except Melanie and where she is and what has happened to her.'

The police say they have asked Mr Simms to remain available for the foreseeable future. Speculation is growing that this is now a murder hunt.

August 12th

How can they write things like that?

She can't be dead, except that's what Daddy's thinking – **he said so!** I don't know what Mum thinks – **maybe she thinks so too!**

But I'm sure Jonah wouldn't have hurt her. Mel said he was the only one she could trust.

She didn't take the things she said she would though, and she hasn't been in touch, even with me. What is wrong with her? She's changed so much, but she still loves **me** – I know she does. **Why won't she answer me?**

Mum and Dad did an interview for all the papers. The police organised it. They said horrible things about Jonah. If they'd been true Mel would never have liked him.

The police are going to start searching for a body now. They told Mum and Dad that they had to – they said it was *the next logical step!* But it didn't mean that they wouldn't find her safe and well.

But if she didn't go off with Jonah what did happen to her?

August 13th

Grandma and Grandpa came again. Gran and Mum went off into the garden to talk. Grandpa took me into town. Dad stayed at home. We went to the park and Grandpa tried to talk about ordinary things, but it didn't work. We talked about Mel and I told him how much I miss her. He says I've got to be very brave. He says he and Grandma will do all they can for Mum and Dad, but I've got to remember they all love me too. He said did I want to go and stay with them for a few days? But I can't leave. I've **got** to be here when Mel comes home.

August 14th

Ali got home from her holiday today. She rang this afternoon to say they were back and to find out what's been happening. We are going to meet up tomorrow.

August 16th
I can't bear to write this. I feel sick. They've found Mel – she's dead.

August 17th
This is the worst day of my life!

I couldn't write any more yesterday. I don't want to write today, but I can't talk to anyone.

Mum's in shock – she had to have the doctor and he gave her some really strong stuff to help her sleep. It didn't do any good, she just went round and round the house all night. She was crying and talking and she just pushed Dad away from her when he tried to help. In the end he went and locked himself away in the study. Then she came to talk to me. She said she wanted to explain things to me, but it was **the middle of the night** when she came. She doesn't even know what time it is!

She said that I had to understand that it wasn't her fault. She said she had always tried to do the best for both of us. She just sat on my bed and went on and on about it until I was sick. Then she had to shut up and do something about that.

I can't think about Mel, but I've got to do something so I'm going to try to write it.

Ali rang on Monday morning – yesterday – to say she was coming round. When the doorbell rang I thought it was her so I rushed to open it. It was the nice police lady, Annie, another police lady and a man. They all looked very fierce. Annie sort of smiled and said they needed to talk to Mum and Dad. They came in just as Mum came out of the kitchen. She looked at Annie and made a funny moaning noise. Annie got hold of her arm and took her into the sitting room. The man asked where Dad was – he had been in the garden so the man went to find him. When they got back into the sitting room Annie got up and got hold of my hand and took me out.

I asked her what was going on, but really I knew – I just didn't want it to be true.

She took me into the kitchen and made me sit down. She said that she couldn't say anything until her friends had talked to Mum and Dad. I didn't say what I was thinking, but she knew that I knew. I told her Ali was coming, so she rang Ali's Mum to tell her not to come. She didn't say why, but I expect they guessed too.

It seemed a long time before she took me back into the sitting room. She kept trying to talk to me about all sorts of stupid things – school, Ali, what I liked doing – **as if I cared**, **as if it matters!**

Mum was sitting on the sofa all hunched up. She was cuddling a cushion – just like Mel does when she's upset about something. She wasn't making any noise, but I could see the tears on her face. She didn't even try to wipe them away. Daddy held out his arms for me – I went to him and gave him a hug, but then I remembered how he always hugs Mel and I couldn't stand it any more.

The man looked at Dad. *Shall I tell her or do you want to?* Dad just shook his head – he didn't look as if he wanted to talk. The man started to explain. He took such a long time I wanted to scream at him.

They had found a body in the woods early that morning. It was buried in the middle where not many people go. They wanted Dad to go and identify it! They keep calling her it. **That's my sister they're talking about.**

Both Mum and Dad went in the end. I don't think they wanted Mum to go, but she insisted. I stayed behind with Annie. She rang Gran and asked her to come straight away.

I sat there feeling more and more sick – just like I do now. Annie kept asking if I wanted a drink or anything, but I couldn't talk.

Grandma and Grandpa got here before Mum and Dad got back, but Annie wouldn't tell them anything. They knew too though – just like I did.

I can't write any more.

August 17th

Missing Schoolgirl: Body Found

Body in the woods

A body discovered two days ago in local woods is believed to be that of the missing schoolgirl Melanie Winters.

The body was discovered by a team of police searching local woodlands in the early morning.

A police spokesperson confirmed that the search had been undertaken as part of their new intensive operation to discover the whereabouts of the missing teenager.

All avenues are explored

'When a young person goes missing,' the spokesperson said, 'our first response is to look for friends who may have information. It was a reasonable first assumption, given that Melanie had gone missing on a previous occasion.

'Our enquiries this time did not bring about the desired result. Once Melanie had been missing for a longer period of time there was a shift in the direction of our enquiries.

'We had originally focused on the fairground communities as information we had received suggested this as a likely possibility for her location.'

Further enquiries

'The decision was taken at the weekend to resume our enquiries nearer Melanie's home.

'It was known that Melanie and her boyfriend met in particular areas of the neighbourhood including the local park and the wooded area known as Lincoln's Copse.'

Although the woods provide several popular walks, some areas are left undisturbed for conservation reasons.

The public is requested not to enter these areas and it was in one of these that the body was discovered. The police have not provided details of the murder, nor have they as yet confirmed that the body is Melanie.

Mr and Mrs Winters were unavailable for comment, but it is known that the police have been keeping them informed.

Melanie Murder: Latest

Identity confirmed

Police have confirmed today that the body discovered in Lincoln's Copse on Monday is indeed that of Melanie Winters.

The body was found during an early morning search, which was part of a routine search pattern, rather than the result of information received.

Asked to confirm identity

Melanie's distraught parents were asked to identify items of clothing and other belongings.

The police have revealed few details of the crime, but have confirmed that Melanie was strangled and that her body was concealed in a part of the woods which is unlikely to have been visited by the many people who use the woods for recreational reasons.

It is understood that the corpse was buried in a shallow grave amongst tree roots. Earth and stones had been heaped over the body and an ivy covered fallen tree trunk had been dragged over the mound to conceal it.

Unexpected find

Police officers involved in the search were alerted to the grave by signs that a tree trunk had been moved. The police spokesperson stated that 'We did not expect this development. The body may not have been discovered so quickly if the searchers had been less thorough. It was very well-hidden and some way away from the public paths.'

Melanie's family have asked to be left alone while they come to terms with the shock of the discovery. A police spokesperson made a statement on their behalf in which they thanked all those involved in the search for Melanie.

Shocked friends and neighbours have visited the house to express their grief and with offers of support for the bereaved family.

The police have confirmed that Melanie's death probably happened within a few hours from the time her father dropped her off at the school gates, a little under a mile away. They have appealed for anyone who saw Melanie on the morning she was last seen to get in touch with them as soon as possible. They hope that someone might have seen her either near the school gates or near the woods.

Focus on friends

The police will be conducting interviews with Melanie's friends in an attempt to help them piece together a picture of her movements on that last fatal day.

August 18th

I couldn't write about everything so I've just stuck in bits from the newspaper. They've given up trying to hide that from me.

There are people hanging around outside the house and I'm not allowed out, so I've come upstairs to write instead. **I can't believe she's really dead.**

Mum and Dad had to go to the police station to identify her clothes. I can't see why – they were her school things and they all had names in.

Mum was in a state when they got home. She kept saying that Dad should have stopped to make sure Mel got into school. Dad started to cry. He said that it wasn't his fault.

It was both their faults – they made her go to school that day when she didn't want to go – if they hadn't she might still be alive!

Then they had to tell the newspapers. They sent two policemen round to talk to

Mum and Dad and get them to think of something they could say. They didn't send Annie this time. They said they would try to do something about the reporters and if they had something to read out to them it might help – they might go away. Some of them went but not all – they want photos of all of us.

It's horrible – how can they want photos of our family when we haven't got Mel to be in them?

They won't tell me about it. Dad says *You don't want to know all the details*. Mum keeps on about how horrible it all is. But I do want to know. Why **WON'T** they just tell me properly? Even Grandma thinks they should tell me everything – I heard her say so – but they won't. It's worse **NOT** knowing 'cos I keep thinking **AWFUL** things.

I have to go downstairs and listen at night – it's not hard, since they keep on and on about it.

She was strangled!

The man who did it used the strap of her purse – he'd looped it round her neck and pulled it tight using her school ruler to wind it round and round. The purse was still on the strap.

She was in a hole made when a big tree fell over – she was covered over with soil and stones and then another old fallen tree had been pulled over the place. There was lots of ivy and stuff all round to make it difficult to see.

They've got to do lots of tests on her body!

They want to know if she was killed straight away. They said it's not going to be easy because the body was **quite badly decomposed!**

Mum tried to talk to me about it today. She said that *I wasn't to worry about myself, they will make sure I'm safe and that the police will catch the man and lock him up for a very long time.* She said that we all had to be together to get through it, but we would in the end. She said it would be better when we could have the funeral, but we wouldn't be able to do that for ages. She said that they are going to have a special service in the church on Sunday and we can all go to that.

I said I was fed up with being indoors and could I have Ali round? She said not yet. The police don't want us to talk to anyone outside the family for a few days. She said they're worried about me talking to the people from the papers. **As if!**

August 19th
Mel was pregnant! I was right! Why didn't she tell us?

I suppose it was Jonah, like I thought. I wonder if she told him – he would have found out soon anyway.

I don't know how the papers found out – I thought the police were keeping everything a secret.

There was a whole lot today about Jonah

Murder of a Pregnant Schoolgirl

Pregnant

Fourteen-year-old Melanie Winters was three months pregnant when she was killed at the start of the summer holidays.

This intelligent, vivacious teenager had been a happy child but reports of her last few months of life tell a different picture.

Personality change

Her friends, shocked by the news of her murder, have told how her personality changed during the early months of the year. 'She didn't want to hang around with us as much.' said one close friend.

Another confided that she knew that Melanie had a boyfriend who was much older. 'She changed. She seemed really unhappy a lot of the time. She got so moody, but she wouldn't tell us what was the matter.'

Her close friends now believe that it was the relationship with this 'boyfriend' which caused Melanie so much anguish.

Calculated abuse

Suspicion is growing that Melanie may have been the victim of a clever paedophile, a man who deliberately fostered an inappropriate friendship with the young girl.

A psychologist who has studied the effects of child abuse explains some of the classic signs and characteristics.

She writes: 'Abused children frequently distance themselves from their close friends. The abuser often grooms the child (develops a non-sexual relationship which may last for months or even years) and forms a close friendship before the abuse starts. The child is convinced that the abuse is a consequence of their own actions and will be reluctant to tell anyone else what is happening.

'The child begins to fear that he or she will get into trouble and fail to realise that it is the adult who would take all the blame.

'Various behaviour patterns may begin to emerge. Often children begin to display traits which are totally unlike their previous behaviour.'

A new view of Melanie

The picture we have put together of Melanie's last months supports this possibility. In Melanie's case it is obvious that the withdrawal from her friends was an indication that something was really wrong. Her changes of mood are evidence of a deep unhappiness, and reports that she was skipping school should perhaps have been a warning to the adults in her life.

The man Melanie referred to as her boyfriend, John Simms, was previously held in custody after a nationwide search, but was released before the discovery of Melanie's body.

— although they didn't write his name. They're saying he was a paedophile. **That's stupid – he was her friend. She said he was the only person she could really trust**. And she said she *hadn't had sex* with him but I suppose she must have.

This has started Mum off again. She got hysterical when the police came to tell us. Annie came again and she asked Dad if she could tell me, and he said yes. She was three months pregnant. I suppose that's why she ran off before – so that she could be with Jonah and we didn't have to know about it.

August 20th
The newspapers say it was Jonah! He's been arrested again!

They are saying all sorts of horrible things about him. Dad was raving mad – he was shouting at Mum and going on about *perverts* and what he would do to Jonah *if he could get his hands on him*.

They are saying Jonah's a paedophile.

Man Arrested in Melanie Winters' Murder Case

Local man in custody again

Police have confirmed that the man in the Melanie Winters' case is again in custody – helping with their enquiries.

John Simms, a local man, has been working for some months as part of the travelling fairground community.

His mother has been settled locally for some years and Simms was educated at the local comprehensive school where Melanie's mother works as a year head.

Simms is described by his mother as 'A gentle person who would never harm anyone. He's not very clever but he's a good boy.'

Wild young man

However other reports paint a different picture. He was a wild youngster who spent more time roaming the local woods, Lincoln's Copse where Melanie's body was found, than attending school.

There have been past allegations of various criminal activities, although none have resulted in conviction.

Simms struck up a friendship with Melanie in the early months of this year and they were seen together at various locations in the district – including Lincoln's Copse.

Unaware she was missing

It is known that Simms left the area in May and he was not seen again until his arrest ten days ago. Melanie disappeared for several days at the end of June, and it was believed at the time that she was with Simms.

The police were informed but she returned to the family home before a search was started.

Simms returned home before the discovery of Melanie's body and was immediately taken into custody. He claimed to have been unaware of the fact that Melanie was missing.

Police have refused to provide further details relating to the murder at this point. They say that to make many of these details public may jeopardise the outcome of any charges they may wish to bring.

That's an old man who has sex with children, but I don't think Jonah could have been one. He's not like any of the things they said. **Anyway, I'm sure Mel wouldn't have liked him if he'd been one of them.**

August 21st
It was the service for Mel today. There were loads of people at the church. I didn't know most of them.

The vicar said really nice things about Mel and so did Mum's headteacher. They went on about what a lovely kind, clever person she had been. It made me cry.

Afterwards I got away from them for a bit and went to find Ali. Her mum gave me a big hug and said that I could go round any time I wanted and no one would say anything about Mel to upset me. I said that Mum wouldn't let me out 'cos of the papers, but she said she'd ring her up and try to get her to change her mind.

Then I couldn't stand it all so I went back into the church all by myself, just to get away from everyone. It was nice in there – I don't know why we ever thought it was spooky. I might go there again when it's open.

I sat there for quite a long time. Until they came and found me. I was thinking about Mel and about all of us. I don't know what's going to happen.

Dad said to Mum we might think about moving *when it's all over*. Mum said she couldn't even think about things like that. She said there's too much still to happen.

She's sure it was Jonah. She's got it all worked out. She says that he must have killed her because she was pregnant. She says he knew that they would get the police involved 'cos that's what they threatened before. She says she *hopes they put him away for ever and never let him out again.*

How could he have done it? Mel trusted him. I hate him!

August 24th

Mum is so cross they've let him go. She says he's fooled them. She doesn't believe his alibi.

The police came round again. **They said that the baby isn't Jonah's!** They've done tests to prove it. They said they had to let him go because *they can't make a case.*

Dad asked what would happen now? They said they've got to start again right from the beginning. They thought it was Jonah too, so they've got to try to find out if she was seeing anyone else.

After they'd gone Mum had a go at me. She seems to think I know something. I said I didn't, but she won't believe me. She said I *'kept things from her before so how can she trust me now?*

I don't see why they keep on at me. Mum keeps crying; then she gets cross with me. They keep on and on asking questions. I told her that I didn't know anything. Mel didn't have a boyfriend. I **don't know** how she got pregnant.

Melanie Winters: Suspect Released – Again!

No grounds at present

John Simms, the prime suspect in the Melanie Winters' murder case, was released again today.

A police spokesperson said that their investigations were continuing but that, at present, they had no grounds for keeping Simms in custody.

'Simms has an alibi for the period of time during which we believe the murder to have been committed,' the spokesperson said. 'However we are keeping an open mind and will be pursuing all leads.'

Back to the woods

'We will be re-evaluating the evidence we have gathered so far and will be revisiting the burial site.'

Although the site has been thoroughly investigated and forensic evidence has been obtained from Melanie's clothing and possessions, the police hope that a further search will provide more clues.

Since the weather has been warm and sunny, it is possible that any additional evidence will be well preserved.

The police will be looking for evidence such as footprints, threads from the murderer's clothing or perhaps the tools he used to scoop out the shallow grave.

They will also be checking to see if people noticed cars parked nearby.

Friends and family

Police also indicated that they intend to talk again to Melanie's friends and family in an attempt to reconstruct her last few hours.

August 25th

They actually let me out today! Ali's mum rang up and said could I go round? She told me about it when I got there. She promised not to let me go out anywhere by myself in case the newspaper people got to me. She said apart from that I could do anything I wanted. She was really nice to me.

I was just glad to get away from Mum and Dad.

They said I wasn't to talk about Mel so I didn't say anything to Ali's mum. Jimmy tried to ask, but she told him off and told him not to bother me.

I told Ali what I know though – not that I know all that much. I couldn't tell her about how she was killed – it makes me cry even to think about it – but I did tell her about Jonah and about the baby. I made her promise not to tell **anyone**, but she's going to ask Jimmy if he knows whether she had another boyfriend.

August 26th

They had another big row today. Mum said Dad doesn't care. I just came upstairs and hid. Mum rang Grandma and I'm going to go and stay with her for a couple of days. There's no point staying here now, and I hate it, so I said I'd go.

August 29th, Bank Holiday

Home again. I wish I could have stayed longer. They said I could if I wanted, but Mum says I've got to come home to get ready to go back to school.

It was OK at Grandma's but they were **too** kind to me. They didn't say anything about Mel but I know they were thinking about her.

August 30th

Went round to Ali's again.

She said that Jimmy says Mel didn't have another boyfriend although there were quite a few boys who fancied her. Who **was** the baby's father?

I suppose the police will find out soon, then we will find out who killed her. Unless it hasn't got anything to do with the baby.

Mum's been fussing about me going out. She says it's not safe. She's still worried about the newspapers too, but they haven't printed anything much about Mel for the past few days. I've told her I won't talk to anyone.

The papers are still going on about how the police can't find out who did it. They are writing loads of stuff about paedophiles and how everyone needs to watch out and be careful! They keep saying that it was definitely Jonah who did it. I hate it all. I don't know what to think.

August 31st
I went back to the church today. **I wish I hadn't!**

It was really hot again – just like it was on Sunday. **It's not fair that it should all be so nice when Mel's dead.**

I went in and sat down. Then I saw someone come in at the door. I thought I ought to hide like before, then I thought I didn't need to 'cos I wouldn't get told off now. But I nearly screamed when I saw who it was.

It was Jonah!

I thought that he might get me and kill me too.

He held out his hands to me and said not to be frightened. He said he just wanted to talk.

He said he wouldn't come close if I didn't want, but he was going away and he had to tell me something before he went.

He said he'd wanted to come to the church to the service for Mel but he couldn't 'cos he'd been locked up. He said he'd seen it on the telly and he'd seen me and that had made him think he ought to tell me.

I asked what ought he to tell me? But he just wanted to say it all in his own way.

When they let him out he came to the house to look for me, but there were too many people around and he was afraid. He's been hanging about each day but he's had to hide from the news reporters and keep out of the way of the police.

He said that he really loved Mel. He said that they'd never had sex and the baby wasn't his – the police had proved it.

Mel was the only girl who had ever been nice to him. She'd had lots of problems and she'd told him **everything.**

I asked him what he meant. He said he couldn't tell me 'cos Mel didn't want me to know. But **he knew all about it – he knew who it was who'd made her pregnant!**

I said he should tell the police but he said he couldn't.

He said he had to get away from here. Some people had thrown bricks through his mum's windows. He said that the papers had made it so he wouldn't be safe. He said he couldn't tell the police 'cos they'd never believe him – he just wanted to get away while he could. He hasn't got his car any more – it broke down ages ago and he couldn't fix it. That was why he'd had to come back on the bus the first time they arrested him. He said he's going to walk until he's miles away – even if it takes a week – then he's going to find his mates from the fair and they will look after him.

I told him about Annie and how nice she was and said he should go and see her, but he said there was no way he was going anywhere near a police station ever again.

Then he said I **had to be careful**. He said Mel was worried about me – **it might be me next and if it was I was to tell!**

He said that Mel had left some messages for me on the computer. She **had** been planning to run away with him. That's why he'd come back – because he hadn't heard anything from her and he was getting worried about what might have happened to her. He said I had to get into the computer – she'd planned to tell me the password when she was safe with Jonah. He didn't know the password.

He wouldn't tell me any more. He was really scared. He said that if anyone knew where he was that they would hurt him. Lots of people have threatened to do horrible things to him.

I thought about Dad.

I thought about what Jonah had told me all the way home. I know Mel trusted him and liked him, but I don't really know him that well. What was it she wouldn't let him tell me? Why must *I* be careful?

What he said about the baby was true though. It wasn't his.

When I got home the police had been again and Mum and Dad were talking about it. They want to come and talk to me again to see if I can give them any more information. They want to know if I know any other boys she was friendly with.

Should I tell them about Mel's message? I wish I could work out the password and find out what she was going to tell me. Will they be cross that I talked to Jonah? Will they be cross I didn't tell them before?

I don't know what to do.

September 1st

Annie came to talk to me again today. There was another lady with her whose name was Ros. She was quite nice too.

Dad went out early this morning. He said he was going to take the car to the garage to get it cleaned so only Mum and I were at home.

Annie said she needed to ask me a lot more questions. She said that Mum was to keep quiet. She said it nicely so Mum wasn't offended, but she said I had to answer everything myself and it was important that I told them the whole truth about everything.

She made me tell her about what Mel had been like and what she had done for months and months.

I had to tell her everything I knew about Jonah. I told her that I'd seen him in the church. Mum got really uptight and started to yell about how stupid I was to talk to him, but Ros shut her up. They said she was to let me tell everything in **my own words**.

I said I didn't believe it was Jonah. I told them that Mel had trusted him. I told them **everything** Jonah had said – everything I could think of about Mel.

She said that they needed to speak to Jonah again. I said that they couldn't 'cos he had gone. I told her that I'd said he ought to come and see her, but how he was afraid. She said that they could protect him and if I saw him again I was to tell him that. They wrote down everything I said. It was ages before they went.

Then Mum had a go at me again. She said she wasn't going to let me go out at all if

I was going to go sneaking around. I told her I didn't sneak around, and, anyway, it was Jonah who followed me!

By the time Dad got home she was in a state. She tried to tell him all about it but she got really muddled. She told him I'd been seeing Jonah too so he wouldn't listen to anything *I* said.

Then she took a load of pills and went off to bed early.

September 2nd

Mum went into school this morning. Dad said she *shouldn't even think about starting back,* but she says she *has to.*

Annie and Ros came back again. There were two men officers with them too. I thought they'd come to ask more questions but they hadn't. They had come to get Mel's computer! I'd told them that Jonah had said that Mel had left messages for me, so I suppose they thought they might be able to get into it and read them.

Dad said *what on earth did they think they were doing?* He was cross. Annie said they wanted to check to see if she'd been in touch with anyone using the Internet. **I never thought of that!**

Annie asked *had Mum told him they'd seen me yesterday?* and he said she had.

She said that *they needed all the background information they could get.*

They had another row tonight. I heard them but I couldn't be bothered to go down and find out what it was all about. **I'm sick of them both. They don't care about me at all.** Now I know how Mel felt.

September 3rd

Mum's been busy all day getting things sorted for school. Dad said he was going to have a clear-out in the study. He looked all cross and worried. I suppose it's because of Mum. He rang up Ali's mum and asked if I could go and see her for the day. He told her that *things were a bit fraught at the moment and*

I could do with a break. Ali's mum said that she would be happy to have me and I could stay the night if I wanted to, so I said that I did want.

September 4th
Ali's dad brought me home after lunch. I said I could come on my own, but they wouldn't let me. They said they'd promised Dad.

Dad had had a big bonfire in the garden. I wish he'd waited for me – he knows I like bonfires. He said he'd had loads of stuff from work that he needed to get rid of. He said he should really have taken it to work for the shredder, but there was too much so he burnt it instead.

September 5th
The police came again. Late this afternoon. Mum wasn't here when they arrived – she'd gone into school again – but Dad was.

They wanted Dad's computer. I don't know why. Mel can't have left any messages on his machine because Dad would never let us use it since he got this new one.

Annie wasn't with them this time. They didn't say much – they frightened me. They just said they needed it *to assist with their enquiries*.

Mum got back just as they were carrying all the stuff out. She asked what was going on, but they said they couldn't tell her. Then they said that they would need to see us all again soon and we were not to go anywhere without letting them know.

I don't know where they think we are going to go – school starts tomorrow. I **was** looking forward to going to Mum's school, but I'm not now. It won't be the same without Mel.

I wish it hadn't happened.

I wish it could all go back to the way it was before.

I can't sleep. I don't know what to do. I'm frightened. It's daylight now, but it's still very early. I have to write because I can't bear to think any more.

It all started very late. I had gone to sleep, but the screaming woke me up. It was Mum. I've never heard her like it before. She screamed over and over again *It's you, It's you*. Then Dad said something and she screamed even more – *You bastard! Your own daughter!*.

I thought she didn't know what she was saying. What did she mean? What does she think was Dad?

Then I knew what she meant. No – not possible! **NOT DAD. No. NO!**

Then she screamed again. Then there was an awful crash and she stopped. Then there were sobbing sounds. I wanted to go and see what had happened, but I didn't dare. I don't want Dad to come. I want to find out about Mum.

I was afraid Dad might come up so I dragged my bed in front of the door. I'm sitting on the bed now. No one will be able to open the door. I wish I had my mobile – I left it with my school bag ready for tomorrow.

There were no more screams. After a while I heard footsteps. Was it Mum? I don't know. I don't think it was. The footsteps came to my door. I didn't say anything. I held my breath as long as I could. My heart was beating so fast. My mouth was all dry. I want a drink. I don't think I can talk. What will I say?

Where's Mum? Why doesn't she come to me? Why doesn't someone say something to me?

She said it was Dad – she thinks **he** killed Mel. Why does she think that? Why would he do that? He wouldn't have hurt Mel. He loved Mel. He loves **ME**! He's never hurt any of us.

Did he hit Mum when she was screaming? Maybe she's got it all wrong and he had to hit her to calm her down. Did **she** hit him? Is he alright? I want someone to come.

Dad is kind. He's kinder than Mum. He doesn't get so cross with us. **Why** would he kill her?

What about the baby? Did she tell him? He would have got angry about that. But it **wasn't** Jonah's. The police said so.

Who's baby was it?

No! Mum couldn't have meant that. Dad loved us. He loved Mel – he wouldn't have hurt her – he wouldn't have done **THAT** to her.

He said he would never hurt me. He said I had to be kind now Mel's gone. He got in my bed. He was just upset. He said so. He told Mum **I** was upset.

It's so quiet now. No screaming. No footsteps. No sobbing.

Where are they? What are they doing?

I can't write any more. Soon I will have to go downstairs. I don't want to do it. I feel sick. **What will I do?**

September 6th

They took my Daddy away today